STAR CIRCLE

Severn House titles by Davis Bunn

The Rowan novels

THE ROWAN
NO MAN'S LAND
STAR CIRCLE

Other novels

PRIME DIRECTIVE
ISLAND OF TIME
FORBIDDEN
THE SEVENTH SPELL

STAR CIRCLE

Davis Bunn

SEVERN
HOUSE

First world edition published in Great Britain and the USA in 2025
by Severn House, an imprint of Canongate Books Ltd,
14 High Street, Edinburgh EH1 1TE.

Paperback edition first published in Great Britain and the USA in 2025
by Severn House, an imprint of Canongate Books Ltd

severnhouse.com

Copyright © Davis Bunn, 2025

Cover and jacket design by Piers Tilbury

All rights reserved including the right of reproduction in whole or in part in any form. The right of Davis Bunn to be identified as the author of this work has been asserted in accordance with the Copyright, Designs & Patents Act 1988.

British Library Cataloguing-in-Publication Data
A CIP catalogue record for this title is available from the British Library.

ISBN-13: 978-1-4483-1551-2 (cased)
ISBN-13: 978-1-4483-1803-2 (paper)
ISBN-13: 978-1-4483-1552-9 (e-book)

This is a work of fiction. Names, characters, places and incidents are either the product of the author's imagination or are used fictitiously. Except where actual historical events and characters are being described for the storyline of this novel, all situations in this publication are fictitious and any resemblance to actual persons, living or dead, business establishments, events or locales is purely coincidental.

No part of this book may be used or reproduced in any manner for the purpose of training artificial intelligence technologies or systems. This work is reserved from text and data mining (Article 4(3) Directive (EU) 2019/790).

All Severn House titles are printed on acid-free paper.

Typeset by Palimpsest Book Production Ltd., Falkirk,
Stirlingshire, Scotland.
Printed and bound in Great Britain
by CPI Group (UK) Ltd, Croydon CR0 4YY

The manufacturer's authorised representative in the EU for product safety is
Authorised Rep Compliance Ltd, 71 Lower Baggot Street, Dublin D02 P593
Ireland (arccompliance.com)

Praise for Davis Bunn

"Impressive . . . Bunn keeps the suspense high"
Publishers Weekly on *The Rowan*

"Swiftly paced with a deep look at how a transition can help heal past personal traumas, Bunn's latest will interest sf readers"
Booklist on *No Man's Land*

"A wild ride"
Kirkus Reviews on *Island of Time*

"A fast-paced, retro-feeling sci-fi mystery. Bunn offers readers a sure guide through his far-future setting . . . A pleasure. This is good fun"
Publishers Weekly on *Prime Directive*

"I absolutely loved this story! *The Rowan* is a powerful political thriller that delves both into sci-fi and fantasy. The result is a mesmerizing page turner"
David Lipman, producer of the *Iron Man* and *Shrek* films on *The Rowan*

"Bunn's imaginative thriller combines propulsive plotting with sharp observations"
Publishers Weekly on *Burden of Proof*

"A stylistically complex work that lends itself to a variety of audiences"
Library Journal Starred Review of *The Domino Effect*

About the author

Davis Bunn's novels have sold in excess of eight million copies in twenty-six languages. He has appeared on numerous national bestseller lists, and his novels have been Main or Featured Selections with every major US book club. Recent titles have been named Best Book of the Year by both *Library Journal* and *Suspense Magazine*, as well as earning Top Pick and starred reviews from *RT Reviews*, *Kirkus*, *Publishers Weekly*, and *Booklist*. Currently Davis serves as Writer-In-Residence at Regent's Park College, Oxford University. He speaks around the world on aspects of creative writing. Davis also publishes under the pseudonym of Thomas Locke.

ONE

Carlton Riffkind arrived at the Hay-Adams Hotel thirty-seven minutes early. He had not been back to Washington DC for nineteen months and three weeks. It felt both wonderful and sad to pass through the hotel lobby, give his name to the restaurant's maître d', and take his place at a coveted window table. The manager and two of the waiters both remembered him, which was good for a nostalgic smile. An unmeasurable number of events had taken place since his last visit. A world of change packed into twenty short months. Being greeted like he still belonged helped bridge the divide. Despite how he had joined the growing community impacted by the rowan tree, Carlton felt as if he belonged. At least for one brief happy moment.

Around the time that Carlton's career began, the Hay-Adams restaurant had been a place to be noticed. Two centuries of movers and shakers had sat where he was now.

The latest generation of Washington power brokers avoided the place like they would a Covid carrier.

Carlton Riffkind, former K-Street lobbyist, Washington insider, and now political pariah, didn't care what others thought and never had.

Which wasn't necessarily a bad thing, since Carlton had joined forces with the new pariahs. The party controlling the White House had secretly declared anyone accepting the rowan's telepathic gift to be enemies of the state.

Carlton had never ingested a rowan leaf. Becoming a telepath had remained, for him at least, a step he would take at some point in the future. But he was going to do this. His wife and daughter had taken the step soon after the rowan first appeared. Early on, Carlton had reasoned someone needed to play the go-between. Which he had, until the current regime declared all telepaths and their allies to be enemies of the state. He and his family had been forced to flee the country, stripped of all power and influence. Declared a pariah himself.

The longer Carlton sat there, the more certain he became that the Hay-Adams formed the perfect setting for his return.

Forty-five minutes later, he signaled a passing waiter and said, 'It appears my guest has been detained.'

The waiter had long since left retirement age in his rear-view mirror. 'Your guest is in politics?'

'Right at the very top,' Carlton confirmed.

The white-jacketed man was not impressed. 'If any of that lot own a watch, it'd be news to me.'

'I suppose I might as well order,' Carlton said.

But that was when two women were escorted to the next table. As they were seated by the maître d', one leaned over and said, 'He's on his way. Four minutes. Less.'

The waiter asked, 'They with you?'

'In a way.'

'You want, I can move the tables together.'

The other woman seated at the nearby table said, 'His guest needs to decide.'

The waiter inspected her for a long moment. 'I know you from somewhere.'

The woman was dressed like the hundreds of young people climbing the power ladders. Dark, modest, suitably expensive. She did not reply.

The waiter turned back to Carlton and asked, 'You OK with the ladies telling you your business?'

'It's not like I have any choice,' Carlton replied.

'Yeah, I believe I've sung that tune myself,' the waiter said.

'One of them is my guest's daughter,' Carlton replied. 'The other is here to record the event. They need to be close at hand. Precisely how close is up to my guest.'

The waiter's expression turned prunish. 'Just what Washington needs. More people telling their betters what to think.'

Valentina Garnier, there to record what was to come, smiled at Carlton. 'Did that man just diss me? I wasn't sure.'

'You ladies enjoy yourselves now. Have a nice meal. Give this gentleman a break.' He walked to the serving station, returned with menus. 'Now I see why you insisted on separate tables.'

As the waiter started away, Vice President Terrance Dale entered the restaurant. Even in a place so accustomed to power and fame, having a VP appear brought the place to a momentary standstill. Then the seasoned crew did as they were trained and pretended it was all part of just another day.

Terrance Dale cut an impressive figure. Aged in his late sixties, Terrance still held the upright strength of his Wisconsin farm heritage. Terrance headed straight for the second table, where the two women were already on their feet. He hugged his daughter Lauren first, then looked down at Val's outstretched hand and said, 'Am I to assume this old man is off your hug list?'

'I didn't know the protocol for embracing VPs.'

'Soon as I figure that out, I'll let you know. One of many reasons why I'm not interested in serving another term.' Terrance Dale embraced Val, then asked both ladies, 'Why aren't you joining us?'

'It needs to be this way, Daddy,' Lauren replied.

'At least for a moment,' Val agreed.

One of the secret service detail took up station by the restaurant's entry. The other man, the agent who had accompanied Lauren Dale to Russia, greeted the two women, shook Carlton's hand, and said, 'Good to see you again, Carlton. Been a long time.'

Terrance Dale complained to his daughter, 'I don't see you for over a year, then I'm supposed to have you stay twenty feet away?'

'Not that far,' Lauren replied. 'Not nearly.'

Val replied, 'This is important. Hear what Carlton has to say. Then decide if you want to invite us over.'

Terrance humphed, retreated to Carlton's table, and allowed the waiter to hold his chair. 'The vice president should be allowed a few perks.'

'No argument there,' Carlton agreed.

'This is worse than the White House,' Terrance said, waving aside a menu being offered by the waiter. 'At least there somebody tells me when I'm being left in the dark.'

'You're not eating?'

'I'm due at some banquet. I'm giving a speech about something. Prize catfish. Overbred cow. Something agricultural.' To the waiter. 'Coffee for me. Black.' He asked Carlton, 'Are you certain there's a genuine reason why they're not seated with us?'

'A good one,' Carlton replied.

'Long as it's good.' He went silent as the waiter set down a steaming cup and retreated. Then, 'Are you folks off the pariah list?'

'No idea,' Carlton replied.

'Probably not,' Val said.

Terrance Dale represented his party's middle path. In his last televised interview, he described those keeping to a centrist position as the quiet ones. Nowadays, he said, they often felt disenfranchised from the direction their party was taking. The current political wars left them adrift. Unable to find their place in the party and the nation they loved. The interviewer had then asked if the vice president was describing his party members or himself.

The president and his advisers had been suitably furious.

Terrance took his time, sipping his coffee, inspecting the room. Then, 'It must be important, for you folks to come out of hiding.'

Carlton did not reply.

'Not to mention how you insisted we meet in such a public place. Which is curious, since the appointment was set wife to wife. Off my official calendar.' Frosty blue eyes inspected Carlton. 'I assume you wanted to choose the time and place of your unveiling.'

Carlton remained silent.

'Which begs the question.' Another sip. 'Are you setting me up?'

Out of the corner of his eye, Carlton saw Terrance's daughter open her mouth to protest. But Val reached over and touched the woman's arm. Lauren's words remained unspoken.

The silent communication was not lost on the VP. He looked at his daughter, then said, 'Answer my question, Carlton.'

'Whether or not you choose to accept our request,' Carlton said, 'you should go straight back and report everything. Including how this meeting was arranged.'

Terrance's softly spoken words carried the threat of an ice blade. 'Are you using my daughter's presence as a goad or a threat?'

Lauren said, 'Come on, Daddy. Really?'

'It's a valid question,' Carlton replied. 'And the answer is neither.'

Val said, 'Given the situation you endure every day, you're right to ask.'

'I can't believe either of you said that,' Lauren said.

'Believe,' Val said. 'Your father has survived four years of a thousand cuts. He represents a segment of voters the president needs to be re-elected. Terrance accepted the position, hoping that he might draw the administration closer to the center path. He failed.' Val met Lauren's gaze. 'They despise him, and they need him. End of story.'

Terrance studied the two women, then said, 'All right. I'm listening.'

Carlton said, 'We want you to run for president.'

TWO

The vice president's thoughtful, disciplined manner was brought to the fore. He took a careful sip. Signaled to the waiter and indicated his empty cup. Nodded his thanks to the refill. When he spoke, it was to Lauren. 'Maybe now's the time when you ladies should join us.'

'Best not,' Carlton said. 'Right now, you can stand up, cross the street, and tell Avri Rowe we did exactly what you suspected. Tried to manipulate you through your daughter's presence.'

A long breath, then, 'You folks are going public.'

'We have no choice,' Carlton confirmed.

Val said, 'General Skarren, head of defense intelligence, and Avri Rowe, the president's chief of staff, put together a secret expeditionary force and attempted to infiltrate our community in northern Canada. The Canadians caught them and did so without losing a soldier on either side.'

'The Canadians are keeping it quiet at our request,' Carlton said. 'For the moment.'

'Skarren and Rowe's team intend to revamp their tactics and try again,' Val said. 'Canada or elsewhere.'

'We can't let that happen,' Carlton said.

'That explains some rumors I've been hearing,' Terrance said. 'About how Canada is no longer an ally. Comments so absurd I've discounted them as just more of the city's rumor mill.'

'They're not rumors,' Lauren said.

Val said, 'If the Canadian public learns of this invasion, if there's a public outcry and a demand for so-called justice—'

Lauren added, 'Which Skarren may actually want to see happen.'

'The government would have a reason to close our northern borders,' Val said. 'Declare Canada an enemy state.'

'They are escalating this into a crisis situation,' Lauren said.

Val said, 'We are going public. Our aim is to try and stop this before it becomes a full-blown international disaster.'

'Whether or not you're with us, we have to act,' Lauren said. 'Please be with us, Daddy. This is me begging.'

Terrance examined each of them in turn, 'Your group suddenly appears after a year of total silence.'

'Eleven months, three days,' Val said. 'We've been busy.'

'You arrange a public meeting through unofficial channels. And do so six months before the Iowa primaries. So you can ask me to run against a man and an administration I have publicly backed for four of the longest years of my life. His campaign chief and my party are pressuring me to remain his running mate. They see us as a winning team. He is expected to enter the convention unopposed.' When the trio remained silent, Terrance demanded, 'Why would I even consider such an option?'

'Two things,' Carlton replied.

'Go on. I'm interested in hearing how this is not entirely idiotic.'

'The war chest for your campaign currently stands at two hundred and fifty million dollars.'

'Cash in hand,' Val said. 'No promissory notes, no overhyped expectations.'

'This is really real, Daddy,' Lauren said.

Terrance held Carlton's gaze. 'Go on.'

'Second, you don't have to win.'

'It would be great if you did,' Val said. 'But winning isn't the primary issue.'

'It's all becoming clear.' Terrance offered a slow nod. 'You want me to become your sacrificial goat.'

'Not at all,' Carlton said. 'We are asking you to pull our nation back from the brink and serve as our voice of reason. The role you've dedicated your life to.'

Terrance corrected, 'I've done so in service to the party and a cause that defines who I am.'

Carlton said as gently as he could, 'If you move on to the global stage, party affiliation becomes less of a factor.'

Val said, 'The current administration is convinced we're a

threat to world order. They have declared war on our community, whether in Canada or elsewhere. Victory at all costs.'

'Skarren and Rowe have put together a secret cadre,' Carlton said. 'They're acting in conjunction with a number of nations and their military and security.'

'People and countries who until recently were counted as our nation's primary enemies,' Val said.

'Innocent lives are at risk,' Lauren said. 'We can't let that happen.'

Terrance studied them in turn. 'There's not enough time to register me. Or form a new political party.'

'Actually, sir, that's already in place,' Val said. 'All fifty states. Say the word and we spring into action.'

'Surprise, surprise,' Lauren said.

Abruptly, Terrance rose to his feet. 'I'll let you know.'

'Daddy, this is beyond urgent . . .'

This time, it was Carlton who lifted his hand and silenced her. 'Thank you so much for even considering this.'

'When my wife told me about this meeting, she warned me it would rearrange our existence. Tilt our world on its axis. Cynthia loves being right.' He asked his daughter, 'Dare I ask about your own plans?'

'I'm serving as your aide.'

'If I agree to this preposterous, outrageous concept.'

'Almost as crazy as your daughter sobering up. Right, Daddy?' Lauren gentled her response with a smile. 'Can I tell Mom you'll be home for dinner?'

'Do my best.' He told Carlton, 'I'll let you know.'

Val waited while Carlton made the appropriate gestures to placate their using two tables and then ordering nothing more than a single coffee. She accepted Carlton's ride to the train station because she had no polite way of refusing. She had not seen her dear friend for over a year. Carlton had been based in some Caribbean backwater, and she had been shuttling between Paris and a backwater of her own. Val knew what was coming, and dreaded it. The sympathy of friends did little except open the wound. Again. Her only hope was that she would not break down and sob in public. It was a meager aim but all she could manage these days when confronted with the love and concern of friends.

But Carlton did not speak during the entire half-hour ride. Even when they became mired in traffic, and the limo's silence weighed heavy, Carlton did not even look her way. When they finally pulled up in front of the station, he checked his watch and said, 'Your train doesn't leave for another hour. Can an old man buy you lunch?'

'Long as you stop with the old.' Val watched him dismiss the driver with an element of very real dread. It was one thing to break down in the limo's relative privacy. And another thing entirely to lose it in Union Station.

She followed him inside and down to what she considered the world's best food court. His destination was a stall that only sold homemade tomato soup and melted cheese sandwiches. While they waited in line to order, Carlton said, 'I think it's best if you go ahead and inform our New York crew. I am fairly certain Terrance will agree.'

She was so relieved with his focus on the day's business that she could have wept. Which was crazy. But still. 'They'll want to know what our alternative is. In case he refuses.'

'I have no idea. Since we've all been closed off for eleven months.' Carlton gestured for Val to order, then asked for the same again. Soup, red Leicester cheese on sourdough, raspberry tea. He paid and took the lead, aiming for the dead center of the public seating area. The high ceiling chamber was beyond noisy. Val found herself mildly lifted by the hope they were staying well clear of the personal.

Carlton confirmed this the instant they were seated. 'Our friends in Canada passed on a message about dreams you've been having.'

'I'm not sure you can call them that,' Val replied. 'Dreams is too mild a term for what's been rocking my world.'

'Leaders of the Canadian team have experienced similar events.'

'Get out of town.'

That was the last they spoke until the meal was eaten and the trays pushed to one side. Carlton resumed the dialogue as if there had been no pause. 'They have no idea what's behind these incidents. They're asking if you can give them a summary, enough so they can be certain you're all on the same page.'

'Why am I hearing this now and from you?'

'An excellent question.' He leaned closer. 'Recently, we've been in regular contact. They talk, I listen. Quick snippets by way of satellite phones or dark web single-use connections. I'm here in Washington because of them.'

The news was enough to push away any final vestiges of her own internal state. For the first time since forever. 'You've approached the vice president on the say-so of our flawed geniuses in Canada?'

He liked that enough to smile. Val found herself missing the man and the life he represented. Carlton's smile rearranged his face, the hour, the impossibility of all she'd endured. It was that potent. 'Only because my wife told me I must. And my daughter. And Connor. And Denton. Who were drawn into our orbit by these very same geniuses. They all consider these conversations to be part of our world's future. My main contact is a young man named Greg Alderton. He describes having glimpses of some huge event linked to the rowan's energy just beyond the horizon. Very tight moments of precise clarity. Leaving them with utter certainty that these elements must happen, and according to a very exact timeline.'

Val nodded. 'That actually ties in with my dreams.'

Carlton glanced at his watch. 'Tell me.'

'They usually happen right at dawn. Which is good, because I can't ever get back to sleep afterwards.' She leaned back, remembering. 'I know this place is very good, very beautiful, even though I don't actually see anything. More like I'm in the company of people who make the slightest moment feel exactly right. And these people, they're not . . . well, actually, they're not people at all. I know that sounds totally off the wall.'

'It does,' Carlton replied. 'And it also mirrors what Greg tells me they've been experiencing. Go on.'

'They try to speak with me, or communicate, but the block we've known for the past eleven months is there. Like a huge wall, and they're trying to break through, and they can't. And then I wake up. It all happens so fast, never more than a few seconds. My heart's pounding, my head . . . I'm filled with this intense feeling of urgency. This huge great need to make something happen before it's too late.'

He nodded slowly, eyes on the unseen distance, both of them now immune to the surrounding din. 'Yours is essentially the same experience as theirs, only described with more eloquence.' Carlton made a process of checking his watch a second time. 'Now to the other matters that have come by way of our Canadian friends.'

'Terrance Dale.'

'You have to understand something. Basically, our conversations are pared down to thirty seconds, a couple of minutes tops. I simply receive a new set of marching orders. Their capacity for casual chit-chat is nil.'

Val sensed a mental shield rising between her and the chaotic din. She was back in full journalist mode. A story was there for her and her alone. The resulting thrill carried an incandescent quality. She said, 'So basically your job is to give legs to their instructions.'

'That pretty much sums up the life I've recently been leading.' Another brief smile, then Carlton asked, 'Do you know the story of the golem?'

'The word, sure. Not much else.'

'In its original sense, the golem was a creature born out of desperate need. The folklore supposedly began with a sixteenth-century Russian rabbi, who used the fable to instill hope during a dreadful time. When God did not answer prayers, the golem would rise up and protect them by using his terrible wrath. The Eastern myth traveled West in Shelley's novel about Frankenstein, and then the writings of Gustav Meyrink.'

'What does that have to do with us?'

'Two issues. Within and without.' He studied her. 'Do you need to be taking notes?'

'When it comes to story, I have an almost eidetic memory.' She matched his stance, leaning forward until their faces were only a few inches apart. 'This is a story, isn't it?'

'My wife and daughter both say it is, and you're the one to

write it. Which has also been confirmed by our Canadian pals.' He tapped his watch, then continued, 'Two issues. First, our team. We've been completely cut off for eleven months and counting. For the moment, let's assume there are reasons. One of which is that our opposition is waiting for a chance to break in. I know that's an over-simplification, and I don't care.'

'Works for me,' Val agreed.

'Eleven months,' Carlton repeated. 'Other than the occasional instruction from our group in Canada, there's been very little if any joint cooperation. And all the while, the opposition led by Skarren and Rowe is gathering strength. They're hunting. Arresting. Carving niches in our protected areas.'

'People are disappearing,' Val swallowed hard. 'Or dying.'

'Which brings us to my point. We need a public figure to serve as our golem. Someone who will create a myth of protection, in order to survive and continue.'

'I don't like that word, myth,' Val said. 'I don't like it one tiny bit.'

'Nor I, and that's not the point. Because of the second purpose. The golem will serve as our buffer. Just temporarily, mind. Because a change is on the way.' Carlton's entire demeanor took on a new force. 'My wife and daughter and these Canadian contacts speak of what they cannot define. But they're certain nonetheless. The coming transition will shift our position on a global scale.'

'In my brief moments of clarity, I've felt the same,' Val said. 'But sometimes I worry my vista remains permanently skewed.'

'If you want the opinion of one old man, that's utterly preposterous, and your dreams confirm this. You have a role to play, and my ladies say your support is crucial to whatever happens next.' Firm, definite, strong. The Carlton of old. The man who had successfully scaled the heights and became a dominant figure in Washington politics. Until he wasn't. 'What is important now is this. Today's golem needs to have a unique charisma. He must mystify. He has to possess a magnetic quality. He has to *arrest* our opponents' attention.'

'Terrance Dale.'

'He's our man. He will shake their complacency, and halt their aggression. Stop them seeing us as an urgent existential threat that must be destroyed. At least momentarily.'

'And if he refuses?'

'He can't.' Carlton rose to his feet. 'And if I have anything to say about it, he won't.'

Carlton walked her back upstairs, and down to where her train was boarding. He reached for her hand. Gripped. Tight. Strong as his gaze. 'Whenever, wherever. But you know that, yes?' Carlton must have seen what he wanted in her gaze, for he released her and added, 'Have a good trip.'

THREE

'We've got nothing at all,' Darren reported. 'Vice President Dale crossed the street on foot. He entered the Hay-Adams restaurant and spent forty-five minutes in conversation with Carlton Riffkind and Valentina Garnier.'

Kelly Kaiser replied, 'You ask me, we've got more than that. A lot more.'

Ever since their first semi-legal foray across the Mexican border, the action that had switched them from Homeland to the nefarious intelligence operation run by the president's chief of staff and the Pentagon's head of military intelligence, Darren Cotton had been Kelly's go-to guy on all research and surveillance. He was calm, steady, and semi-brilliant at both gathering intel and managing his team of nineteen, plus any number of satellite operatives they could call upon at a moment's notice. Darren still claimed he missed fieldwork. But the protests were muted now, especially as his wife was pregnant with their second child. Not to mention how his counterpart, Barry Riggs, was trapped inside a Canadian military prison, along with all his force, awaiting extradition. Kelly went on, 'I had no idea Riffkind and Garnier were back in-country.'

'Neither did we.'

'I thought their names and passports were flagged.'

'They are.'

'Find out how and when.'

'On it.'

'If they're traveling using false papers, we have the perfect reason to arrest and hold them,' Kelly said. 'Back to Dale.'

'We could have easily set up surveillance if we had known about the meeting,' Darren said. 'Which we didn't. Nothing in his diary and no word to his PA, who passes everything through Avri Rowe's office.'

'Carlton's wife and Mrs Dale are friends,' Kelly recalled. 'That's probably how they kept it off the books.'

'So like I said, we've got nothing to report. Oh, and Lauren Dale was also present. She and Garnier sat at one table, Carlton and the VP at another. But the conversation was between all four.'

'What about that agent on Dale's security team who's bound to be part of the opposition?' And who Dale personally ordered off inactive roles and assigned his head of security. When Avri objected, Dale offered to resign. Avri had no choice but to back down. The administration could not risk a public spat bringing their mutual loathing into the public eye. Especially not six months before the primaries got underway.

'Jadyn James,' Darren said. 'He walked over with the VP. Greeted the three like long-lost pals. They chatted together for a minute. Less. Then he retreated and took up station with the other agents. Even if he wanted, which he doesn't, James can't tell us anything.'

Again, Kelly thought there was a lot to learn from even this brief encounter. They had been wondering for months if the enforced silence her team had endured was an event shared by everyone infected by the rowan tree or whatever it was. If Jadyn and the others were in telepathic communion, taking time for such a public reunion made no sense.

And then there was the other thing.

'Val Garnier and Lauren Dale did not sit with the VP?'

'The tables were inches apart. But separate. Doesn't add up.'

Kelly had several responses to that. But before she could speak, the door leading to the inner office opened and Rabbit stepped out. 'I have to go,' Kelly said.

'Wait, there's more.' Darren's words accelerated. 'Carlton and Val Garnier traveled from this meeting to Union Station. They ate lunch downstairs in the food hall. Again, no way to establish last-minute surveillance. Val took a train to New York, Carlton went straight to the VP's private residence. We have a team on their way to Grand Central. Arrest or surveil, your call.'

'Tell them to hold back and observe. We need to determine their motives for reappearing.' Kelly motioned for Rabbit to join her and told Darren, 'Call you back in one hour. Try and find out how those two entered the country unnoticed.'

The young man who seated himself across the therapist's small lobby from Kelly was very different from the Rabbit who had guided them across the Mexican border. He still wore the same rectangular spectacles with their heavy black frames. His hair was still cut so short he could semi-control it with his fingers. Otherwise, the Rabbit from nineteen months ago was utterly transformed. Nowadays, all the newcomers to Kelly's team referred to him by his real name, Stanley Kuiper. Kelly thought it better suited the man Rabbit had become.

Just the same, Rabbit liked how the original crew still called him by the nickname, a label they had used before Kelly's boss had allowed Rabbit to reveal his identity.

Rabbit now resembled a feral beast. Narrow body, cavernous features, and a tightly compressed rage that radiated through his supposed calm. He stretched out his legs in a semblance of ease and asked, 'How's it going?'

These days, between them, it was as close to intimate as either came. Kelly replied, 'So-so. You?'

'So-so works for me.' Rabbit pointed to the inner office. 'Vivienne needs a minute. Crisis call.'

'No problem. Far as I'm concerned, she can take all day.'

Rabbit mimicked the therapist's mellow drone. 'Humor. Excellent. A good sign of progress.' He stared at her. 'How are you faring?'

'Some days are better than others.' Kelly pointed at the wall behind her head. 'She helps. Some. As much as can be expected.'

Another nod. 'Nights?'

'Ditto. Last week, I started cutting back on my meds. Some. Not a lot.'

'Me, that'd be a bridge too far,' Rabbit said. 'I'd be permanently banished to the sofa.'

The three of them, Rabbit and Kelly and Rabbit's life partner Diyani, had led the first telepathic crew working on behalf of the nation's intelligence service.

Until they couldn't.

Their final operation as telepaths had involved a missile strike against their opponents fleeing over the Canadian border in a stolen plane. The action had been deemed a success, in that the plane was shot down. But the outcome had been personally and professionally disastrous. Every telepath involved in the operation had instantly lost their ability to link.

As soon as they had at least partially recovered, Kelly and Rabbit began assembling a new team of telepaths. They were making solid progress toward establishing a protocol defining their objectives. Several of the opposition had been caught up in sweeps.

Then disaster struck yet again, this time in the form of a blanket silence. For the past eleven months, not even their new telepathic team members could monitor what their opponents were up to. They still had no idea why.

Their leaders' response to this utter lack of intel was a high-stakes gamble. Infiltrate a heavily armed squad across the northern border. Invade the only telepathic community they were certain even existed. Bring back live telepaths for questioning, and send their Canadian neighbors a message. It was time to choose sides.

Kelly carried the mortal agony of a field amputation after losing her telepathic abilities. For the two lovers, Rabbit and Diyani, the effects had gone deeper still.

Kelly asked, 'How is Diyani?'

Rabbit stretched, linked hands behind his head. As relaxed as either could manage these days. 'Where Diyani came from, everything she experienced in the trek north, those events permanently scarred her. It left her expecting very little from life. She's a champion when it comes to enduring the impossible.'

Kelly actually liked this exchange. Being open. Despite everything. 'In a way, I share that with Diyani. Enduring the impossible. You know about Nathan.'

'Your late fiancé. Barry told me. A little.'

'Nathan was killed in Juarez. He was part of that first recce south of the border. His death was what brought you and me together.'

'Whoa.'

She nodded. 'I was alone long before we lost the ability to connect.'

'Kelly . . .'

Rabbit's response was cut off by the connecting door opening. Vivienne Grace offered them both a professional smile. 'Kelly, my sincere apologies.'

'No problem.' She rose to her feet and told Rabbit, 'It's good to catch up.'

FOUR

'I want to talk about this absence of communication. How are your crew handling this?'

Vivienne Grace started all their sessions in such a manner. A direct statement or question, jumping straight into the deep end. She was a dark-skinned woman and large in a solid, muscular fashion. Vivienne had been a federal agent who had completed three university degrees, first in night school and then with her full-time graduate studies financed by the government. Her office was in Pentagon City, five blocks from Kelly's new headquarters. Vivienne only worked with patients who had served – police, intelligence, armed forces, even a few private contractors. She was booked solid. But Rabbit's situation had, as she put it, severely shaken her world. So she had also made room for Kelly, but on two conditions. Vivienne would work with her, so long as Kelly entered her office ready to work. And for the first month, they were to meet every afternoon.

Kelly replied, 'Rabbit could give you a better read.'

'He sees this from an analyst's perspective. But you are their de facto leader.' Vivienne occupied her space with the ease of a somnolent bear. Totally aware, totally focused, totally relaxed. A resting power. She was also one of the most intelligent people Kelly had ever met. 'A good leader, by definition, must maintain a broader perspective.'

Kelly had no idea where the woman was headed. Which was another common trait of their time together. Vivienne asked a series of seemingly disconnected questions, weaving her circular web, drawing Kelly onward without revealing her destination. It was only afterwards, when Kelly was seated in her car and recovering from yet another raw exposure of her dark corners, that she saw the full pattern.

Hard and painful as many of their sessions were, Kelly liked her time here. There was none of the typical glad-handing calm she'd so despised with her other therapists. Vivienne was in-your-face direct, almost aggressive in her softly spoken probing. It said to Kelly that the therapist was totally there. In this. With her.

Kelly replied, 'As far as Rabbit's team are concerned, we're treating this lack of communication as a temporary event.'

Another quick note. A few words, nothing more. Vivienne did not record her sessions. It was part of the confidentiality she promised on day one. 'Even though they can't operate. Engage. Offer life-saving analysis. Because they have all been rendered blind by this blockage to their abilities.' She paused for emphasis. 'Are you certain this is not just offering yourself and Rabbit's team false hope?'

'I am. Yes.'

'Tell me why.'

This was the upside to Kelly's daily sessions. Being able to open up, not just to her therapist. To herself. Question and doubt and inspect her decisions. 'Because our secret contacts within their organization confirm our opponents are blind as well.'

Kelly had almost given up hope.

Three analysts, three strike-outs. She was surviving on anti-depressants and more booze than she had ever drunk in her life. Every chance she had, Kelly drove to Roanoke and retreated into her former fiancé's home, where she was coddled and shielded by Nathan's over-protective mother. Who loved having Kelly to take care of. The hollow void caused by Nathan's murder remained there in the older woman's gaze. She did not need to know what had happened to Kelly, except that she had survived, and she was hurting, and she needed the sort of care Nathan's mother could not give her son.

Nathan's father, a retired Marine colonel, had always considered Kelly the daughter they never had. She was welcome, regardless of her state, or how some nights she hid behind a curtain of booze and pills. Nathan's father had seen his share of good Marines damaged by PTSD, which he assumed was Kelly's situation. Nothing she shared about her own specific events, and she told them everything, changed his perspective. He accepted her tale of becoming a telepath, attacking the enemy, then losing her ability with the severe force of a mental amputation. All he said after her confession was, 'Crippling battleground injuries aren't always visible. You rest. You heal. We're here for you.'

Only she didn't. Heal.

Then Rabbit told her about this new therapist.

Three weeks earlier, Kelly reluctantly walked the five blocks from their new headquarters to Vivienne's office. And there in her first session, Kelly met a woman who did more than listen. She entered into the situation and lived with her. And did so without conditions. Vivienne's attitude said, *I'm hungry to learn. Teach me. Let's walk this road to recovery together.*

Now Vivienne demanded, 'Can you say for certain they have lost their telepathic abilities?'

'All evidence we have gathered confirms these confidential sources. Our opponents have reverted to using satellite phones, dark web one-time sites, and burner phones. I can't tell you more. But our secret contacts are certain, just as we are, that this situation won't last. It can't.'

'I find this very interesting,' Vivienne said. 'The confidence you have in this analysis. Because I see nothing about what you've said that leads to such a straight-line conclusion.'

'It's one of the few points all of Rabbit's team are solid on. There might not be direct communication between any team member, theirs or ours. But everyone in Rabbit's group feels a growing sense of, well, pressure is as good as any term. I'm surprised Rabbit hasn't said anything about this.'

'Whatever Rabbit and I discuss must remain outside the parameters of your and my time together,' Vivienne replied.

'At first, I put these reports from Rabbit's team as false hopes. But what they say is too definite. Too constant. And it's totally in parallel with what we're hearing from inside the opposition. They describe it as watching this great river push up against a dam. Rising to where water is now lapping over the top. The pressure they feel is immense.' Kelly hesitated, then added, 'In the past week or so, the new members of Rabbit's team have started catching brief glimpses now and then. Just the same, it gives me hope.'

'Hope for yourself as well? You ingested a leaf just like Rabbit and his team. Do you not feel the same?'

'Not at all. Nor do any other team members who were linked when we attacked the plane.' Kelly hesitated, then added, 'I get these little shards of dreams. Never more than a couple of seconds.'

'Amputees often experience a temporary sensation of their limbs being restored.' Vivienne leaned forward. 'What makes you certain these dreams are not merely your subconscious mind's attempt to deal with the trauma?'

'Maybe it is. Which is basically why I haven't mentioned it before. But I think it's more.'

'Tell me why.'

'Because every time it happens, I'm blasted from sleep. The feeling is, well, it's beyond great. For one tiny instant, I'm back. Reconnected. And after . . .'

'Yes? Go on.'

'I'm left with a gut-level certainty that what we've heard from our secret allies among the opposition, and what Rabbit and his team occasionally sense, is correct.' Kelly felt the acidic heat rise with her words. A brief glimpse into the cauldron Kelly carried with her everywhere, every moment. A sniper focused on the unseen target had nothing on her. 'Someday soon our opponents are going to re-engage. And when that happens, we'll have our target. And we will go in weapons hot. And we will destroy them.'

Vivienne made another note. Then she set her tablet and pen on the coffee table to her right. The therapist's office was segmented into thirds. A desk of pale maple and a matching office chair faced the side wall. By the opposite wall, up close to the large window with its beige veil of a curtain, was a leather therapist's lounge and Eames chair. Dominating the room's heart were two matching conference chairs and side tables, the space between them open. Revealing. Without barriers or space where the patient might hide. To select this position in the room was to accept the therapist's challenge.

Vivienne said, 'I want to talk about a mental response trait called paranoid personality disorder. Have you ever heard of this?'

'No.'

'PPD describes a pattern of behavior we see all too often in patients recovering from post-traumatic stress. An individual suffering from PPD lives in a constant state of readiness for attack. They are always on guard. They believe others, often a specific group, are continually threatening to harm them. Habits of blame and distrust gradually extend outwards from these poisonous seeds. If not checked, PPD can eventually stifle the individual's ability to form any close relationship—'

'That doesn't describe my situation at all.'

This marked the first time Kelly had come out in opposition to Vivienne's proposed direction. Always before, no matter how much it had cost her, Kelly had given the therapist's suggestions careful thought. Taken them in deep. Considered them for days.

Not now.

'We are dealing with an enemy of the state.' Kelly liked how her voice had taken on the preternatural calm that dominated her world before action. Her heart rate had slowed to somewhere around fifty beats per minute. Her entire body was in a state of temporary repose. Muscles relaxed. This was the point at which Kelly felt most alive, waiting in utter alertness, poised to strike as soon as the target was identified. 'This is not some fake totem I've designed because I need it, or want it, or think it will help ease me through this awful phase. I am part of a team whose leadership stands at the very top of our nation's government. We are dealing with an enemy that might very well defeat us. We are doing our utmost to combat a rising tide that threatens our nation's existence.'

Vivienne waited a very long moment. When she was certain Kelly had finished, she said, 'My point is simply this. An alcoholic who is also suffering from PPD could very well enter recovery, stay sober, but also become an angry teetotaler. Anyone who drinks even a drop of alcohol is viewed as their enemy.'

There was no reason why Kelly should have felt the crawl of electric worms burrow under her skin, through her gut. 'I haven't had a drop since our second session.'

'That's not where I'm going with this, and I think you know it. You can apply this same principle to any number of cases where the patient's traumatic experience has potentially wrecked their existence, forever altered their life's pattern. In the process of recovery, they become hide-bound in the opposite direction. You understand that term, hide-bound?'

'Of course.'

Vivienne said it anyway. 'Their thinking is framed around a rigid interpretation of black and white. They become obsessively attached to a new perspective. They view everything that happens through this lens. Rage is part of their world now, their every waking moment. They seek an opportunity to apply this fury, to direct it at anything they consider an enemy. PPD is a side-bar, a natural outgrowth of this perspective.'

The electric worms burrowed deeper. Invading her brain to where she could almost feel them threaten to fracture her thoughts. Her vision. 'My response is the same.'

Vivienne continued as if Kelly had not spoken, 'This in itself creates a weakness. Underneath, there is a growing vulnerability. The patient is often not aware of this, at least on the surface. But down deep, where it matters most, the rage serves as a shield against what they have not managed to resolve. And as a result, this skewed perspective on what they view as reality carries a genuine threat. They hold the potential to damage and destroy, most especially to themselves and those closest, which is precisely what brought them into therapy in the first place.' A pause, then, 'Do you see where I am headed with this?'

Kelly did not respond.

'What we need to uncover, what I want you to consider between now and our next session, is this. Who is the real enemy here? Are they out there, or are they actually down deep inside yourself?'

Kelly remained silent.

'Unless there is a true healing, the threat of damaging the innocent is very real. An alcoholic who has not resolved their internal crisis points remains simply an alcoholic who does not drink. A soldier returning from the battlefield who does not acknowledge the threats associated with PPD feels threatened by everyone who comes close. There is a very real risk that some unexpected event, or a pattern of behavior by someone beyond their tight control, will trigger a violent and destructive rage. This black-and-white perspective threatens to demolish their existence and wreak havoc in every relationship. I can't say whether the same applies to you. Only you can determine whether this is truly an issue. Which is why I feel it's important you at least consider this between now and our next session.'

Kelly did not speak.

'Do you perceive those who still have the ability you've lost, the ones who have not suffered this mental amputation, from such a black-and-white perspective? Do you find comfort in isolating yourself among people who share this point of view?' Vivienne's words held a soft drumbeat of inevitability, pounding into Kelly's turbulent brain. 'Do you risk wreaking huge damage on the innocent by not fully considering alternative perspectives?'

The clock on Vivienne's desk gave a soft ping. After some sessions, Kelly felt as if the sound carried the force of an ice pick to her brain. Just like now.

Vivienne rose to her feet. 'I would simply ask that you consider this possibility until we next meet.'

FIVE

Val found it both strange and oddly comforting to be arriving back in New York City. She had never actually lived here. Her home, such as it was, had always been Annapolis. But her professional life as a journalist had revolved around Manhattan – publishers, magazine headquarters, the heartbeat of professional writing remained here. Back before her world tilted on its axis, she used to take the Acela north every couple of weeks. Watching the train pull into Grand Central for the first time in over a year and a half, everything seemed both normal and very new.

When she stepped off the train, the security detail Connor Breach had assigned her was waiting. Val thought it was probably overkill. Just the same, it felt good to be somewhat insulated from the threats Val knew were both very real and very close.

Even in such totally bizarre circumstances, Val loved being back in the Big Apple. Her security team drove a black GMC with a back seat that could sleep six. She settled in, declined their offer of a coffee for the ride, confirmed the destination, and watched the city unfold. Val had not been back since unseen forces had stifled her articles and vacuumed up every shred of evidence that the rowan's gift of telepathy ever existed.

The guard in the front passenger seat was a dark-suited woman in her late thirties or early forties. Stocky, raven hair cut very short, toneless manner of speech. British accent. She reached back and said, 'This is for you, Ms Garnier. Compliments of Denton Hayes.'

'Can I ask your name?'

'I'm Lynda Eliott, ma'am.' She indicated the driver. 'And this gentleman is so utterly bland I am often at a loss to remember he's there at all.'

'The name is Samuel, ma'am. And it's a pleasure.'

'An auto-driving software would have more personality,' Lynda said, smiling at their driver.

'That will cost you,' Samuel replied.

Val made no move to accept the phone and charger. 'I bought a burner phone in DC.'

'This is a next-gen sat phone. The numbers for Mr Hayes and Ms Breach are taped on the back.'

The days when communicating with allies and friends had been a simple act of thought or emotional direction were over. Had been for eleven months and counting. She accepted the phone and charger and stowed them in her purse.

The guard continued, 'It works like a regular phone. Button on the top turns it on. Automatic encryption when you're chatting with a like-minded device. Very impressive bit of kit.'

Samuel offered, 'Five thousand bucks is what I heard.'

Lynda nodded. 'Not something you can pick up at your local news stand, that's for certain.'

They drove south and were soon mired in lower Manhattan traffic. Seven blocks and twenty minutes later, Lynda fretted, 'We're growing increasingly behind schedule.'

'If you have an idea how to speed things up,' the driver replied, 'I'm open to anything that doesn't involve gunfire.'

Lynda turned around. 'Ms Garnier, you mind walking?'

'It's Val. And I'd relish the chance to stretch my legs.'

'The car is safer,' Samuel said.

'You heard the orders same as me. Timing is crucial.' Lynda pointed to a fire lane. 'Pull in there, text me when you arrive.'

The late September air was dense with diesel-laced humidity, the sky overhead blanketed by clouds. Just the same, it felt good to be out and moving. The guard set a pace one notch off a jog, flowing with liquid ease through the heavy foot traffic. Five blocks later, they entered a new high-rise, part of Wall Street's encroachment north. Val showed her ID to the reception guard, who phoned ahead, then issued temporary passes and buzzed them through. The elevator had no buttons. They emerged into the lobby of a firm large enough to claim the entire floor. The wall opposite the elevator held the copper-plated name, Cotton Southerns.

Val knew another internal tightening at the sight of Denton Hayes and Connor Breach. Perhaps she would grow accustomed to the kind words of friends. But just now every such meeting carried the threat of opening her unseen wounds. Especially when the two of them lost their smiles the instant she emerged from the lift.

Just the same, both showed a very professional courtesy. They didn't bother to ask how she was, or whether she was managing to hold her life together. Such as it was. Connor offered a lightning-fast embrace; Denton shook her hand, said it was good that she could join them. As if any of them had been given a real choice in the matter.

Val had any number of questions she wanted to ask, starting with why she needed to be here at all. But the receptionist was already on his feet, and Connor told the woman, 'We're ready to proceed.'

'Right this way.'

They followed the young man down a side corridor and into a corner conference room. The view was spackled by the day's first raindrops, but still awesome. Val watched a tourist boat trundle along the East River and wished her days could include such idle hours. And that her heart wouldn't use them for just another opportunity to mourn what was no more.

The conference room held two women. One was in her mid-fifties, give or take five years either way. She was dressed in a dark grey suit that perfectly matched her eyes, which were as toneless as the sky. Not angry so much as perpetually impatient. 'You've kept us waiting almost twenty minutes.'

'My sincere apologies.' Connor Breach was the exact opposite of the senior attorney, but running along a parallel track. Two lawyers with contrasting personalities. One constantly on edge, the other calmly resolute. Both intensely intelligent. And already sparring. 'We were unable to proceed without our associate, Valentina Garnier.'

The hard grey eyes swiveled over, then back. 'What role does a journalist play in these proceedings?'

'We need to maintain an ongoing record.'

'A public record. Of your initial meeting with a trial attorney.'

'Correct.'

'That is hardly normal in my line of work.'

'I doubt very much what we are here to discuss has anything to do with your definition of normal.'

The attorney was not impressed. 'I charge double for time wasted.'

'Understood.' Connor slipped around the table and seated herself with her back to the windows. Denton selected the chair to her left, Val on her right. The attorney took a seat directly opposite them and passed around cards declaring her to be Rachel Bernstein, partner. Her younger associate was Consuela Almeida, silent, attentive, equally intelligent. Connor said, 'We don't have cards made up yet.'

'You've established a retainer with our accounting department,' Rachel said. 'That will do for the moment. Though I must warn you, I haven't yet agreed to take this case.'

'There is no case,' Connor replied. 'Hopefully, there will never be.'

'You're not making any sense.' The conference table was palest maple, the chairs doeskin and steel. Two very nice Miró prints occupied the wall behind the in-house attorneys. The conference room held no shelves of untouched law books, no power wall. Everything stated very clearly that this place and these people were all business. No nonsense, no overblown egos, no visible courtroom brawls. A thousand bucks an hour for the partner, five hundred for her younger associate. The clock was ticking. 'Why are we meeting?'

'My associate, Denton Hayes, has been appointed deputy ambassador to the United Nations for the nation of Grenada.'

Bernstein inspected them in turn. 'Assuming this is legitimate—'

'It is. Very.'

'In that case, you apparently are not aware that I am strictly involved in litigation.' When Connor did not respond, she continued, 'That's all I do. I litigate. I go into the courtroom, and I fight for my clients and their interests. You need one of those firms further uptown.'

'We're precisely where we need to be,' Connor replied.

But Bernstein wasn't done. 'Their conference rooms look like an English manor's library. They wear nice suits. They'll bring you tea in a silver service.' To her assistant, 'Go dig up the addresses—'

Val broke in with, 'As soon as Homeland knows Denton is here, and what he intends on doing, they will do their best to make him disappear.'

Bernstein leaned back. When she remained silent, her associate said, 'They can't do that.'

Denton spoke for the first time. 'Can and will.'

'They will claim our new passports and citizenships are all a sham,' Connor said. 'Illegal usurping of national sovereignty.'

Bernstein demanded, 'Is it?'

'Absolutely not.'

Denton said, 'We have acquired the right to co-represent their island nation. We have also established a separate treaty-state on one of their previously inhabited islands.'

'You've *acquired*,' Bernstein said. Without lifting her hand from the table, she pointed one finger at her associate. Immediately, Consuela Almeida pulled a yellow legal pad and pen from her purse and began taking notes.

'Or leased, if you prefer,' Denton said.

'Ten thousand dollars to every adult citizen of Grenada,' Connor said. 'Fifty million more to the central government.'

That froze both attorneys. Finally, Bernstein managed, 'What on earth . . .'

'Per year,' Denton said.

'This is real, this is happening,' Connor said. 'And Homeland will do everything in its power to make us disappear.'

Consuela said, 'But *why*?'

'I will not be party to a semi-legal attempt to smuggle drugs,' Bernstein snapped.

'This is nothing of the sort,' Denton replied.

'No drugs, no contraband, no arms, no violent gangs, no illegal shipments of any kind,' Connor confirmed. 'If you have any reason to suspect otherwise, at any point, you are welcome to walk away.'

'Until then, we want one of your associates to shadow our

every step,' Denton said. 'Close as my next breath. There to witness our arrest. And fight for our immediate release.'

'Arrested on what grounds?'

Connor replied, 'We assume it will be the Prevention of Terrorism Act.'

Denton checked his watch, signaled Connor, and rose to his feet. 'We are scheduled to meet the Grenada embassy staff in twenty-seven minutes. You or your associate should join us. That will clear things up.'

'As clear as things can be at this point,' Connor said.

Bernstein asked the younger attorney, 'What's on our agenda after this meeting?'

'Partner's conference in twenty.'

'Cancel.' She rose to her feet. 'You and I are going uptown.'

SIX

They traveled in three vehicles. Denton insisted that Val keep her limo for the next portion of her day's journey. What that might be, he did not say. Denton and Connor traveled together in an identical SUV with their own guard detail. Which was not lost on the two lawyers.

Their journey took less than twenty minutes. For once, the cross-town traffic was moving well. The Permanent Mission of Grenada to the United Nations was located on Second Avenue, within easy walking distance of the UN Plaza. They parked in the No Waiting zone that fronted all UN consulates. Denton had obviously called ahead, because they were instantly buzzed through the security barrier and greeted by a sullen woman who did not introduce herself. They followed her upstairs and into a long narrow meeting room that barely held all seventeen staff members.

Denton asked if the ambassador was joining them. No one responded. At a gesture from Denton, Connor made her way around the table, apologizing as she nudged through the compressed group. While she set up a portable AV projector and connected it to her phone, Denton introduced each of their group, including the attorneys. The Grenadians remained grim, angry, suspicious. Silent.

Connor said, 'Ready at this end.'

'My name, as I said, is Denton Hayes. This talk was supposed to be given by a gentleman from Martinique, Dr Bernard Severant, this woman's late fiancé.' He pointed at Val. 'For the moment, we are accepting the French police report giving his reason for death as a heart attack. Which is true as far as it goes, since every life ends when the heart stops beating.'

The woman who had escorted them upstairs spoke for the first time, her anger spiced by the musical Caribbean lilt. 'You're putting us all at risk, you being here. That's what you're saying.'

The man seated next to her said, 'No bribe is big enough to pay for killing just one of us.'

'If anyone in this room faces such a threat, we will end our connection immediately—'

The woman demanded, 'What kind of drugs are you transshipping through our country; that's what I want to know.'

'No drugs, no guns, no gangs,' Denton quietly replied.

'And all you want for all this money is a rock island with no harbor, no beach, and no fresh water?'

The woman's words released a volcanic spewing of angry words from many encircling the table. Denton stood and waited them out. Finally, the woman raised her voice loud enough to be heard. 'Oh, let the man speak.'

'You have every right to be both scared and angry. I wish Bernard were the one talking to you. He would do a much better job. But I'm all you've got. So here is my request. We ask that you watch a twenty-two-minute video the lady seated here to my right has prepared. We will be leaving a written summary of what you will be viewing. Valentina Garnier is a Pulitzer Prize-winning journalist and authored the report as well as shot most of the video's raw footage. It is her voice you will be hearing.'

Their spokeswoman demanded, 'And if we don't believe? If we listen and we read and we watch and we still want you gone?'

Denton's sheer exhaustion showed through. 'I have no answer. Your government has granted us a year. We are in a desperate situation. Without you people on our side . . .' He shook his head, then told Connor, 'Go ahead and pass around the article.'

The video was a much more professional version of the material originally put together by Richie Bond, and included footage Val and others shot of the two rowan trees, their impact, and the second rowan tree's destruction by a Tomahawk missile. Val and a team in Zurich had been working on it for almost two months. Ever since the communique had arrived by way of Denton Hayes, but originating from the tight-knit Canadian team with no name.

Over the past year and a half, groups made up of those once considered disabled had coalesced in northern Canada. So many they effectively pushed out everyone not involved in their care and their operation. The absence of protest from those expelled from the settlement was somehow reassuring.

Then, eleven months ago, the bonds linking all telepaths were severed.

Throughout this silent period, certain messages still emerged from this one group.

Most of these communications had to do with investments. As a result, the groups' holdings had ballooned out of all proportion to their needs. Billions were now available at the touch of a keypad. People assigned responsibility for managing these funds had established numbered accounts in every country specializing in confidential banking. Every island.

Denton was one holder of these accounts. Richie Bond. Connor Breach. Camila Suarez was head of their investment team. Val. About a dozen others. Not many, considering how their assets now totaled more than the cash reserves of many countries.

Other than these occasional snippets of instruction, the Canadian group remained silent. Utterly enclosed. Cut off from the outside world.

Until two months ago.

Recently a new string of non-investment communications had emerged. Most of these arrived by way of one-time peer-to-peer dark web sites. A very few instructions were also passed on by two and sometimes three separate satellite phone messages. The group remained very careful. Almost paranoid. And always with a very tight timeline.

Denton's team had been ordered to develop a professional-grade video presentation, with Valentina Garnier writing and then delivering the overdub. The Canadian group specifically named Val as the one who must take responsibility for this.

Then an utterly different kind of message emerged from this otherwise silent community. They reported that Agnes Pendalon's top-secret team of agents were entering Canada. Heading north. An invasion force aimed at their community. The message's timing was as precise as the insistence that they be stopped without any loss of life. Thankfully, there were now enough allies within the Canadian government to make this happen. The US squad's communications were jammed, then they were surrounded by a huge and overwhelming show of force. The US agents surrendered without a shot being fired.

Since that took place, the global group's focus gradually shifted. Every communication between friends, allies linked in secret chatrooms, virtually all their discussions centered upon one new experience they all now shared.

Pressure.

Something was about to happen. A series of events that would transform their existence. Bigger than everything that had happened so far.

It was then that the Canadian group sent out the most bizarre communications of all.

First: enlist the help of Grenada. The island nation's prime minister and three members of her cabinet belonged to their community. Agree to whatever terms they set out.

Second: ask Terrance Dale to run for president of the US on an independent ticket. Do everything to make this a reasonable, valid request. Money no object.

Third: Val and Denton and Connor must set aside their anonymity and travel to New York. Shield themselves legally for the confrontation to follow.

At least, Val assumed those were the last orders to emerge. But what did she know? After all, she was merely a pawn in this game. And a damaged one at that.

Val spent much of the video studying the room. Regardless of her semi-wrecked internal state, she was still, first and foremost, a journalist. Observation was the foundation of her job.

Val could see she faced a tight-knit cluster of professionals. Their primary task in New York was to pursue as much power and money as possible – especially money. They might only gain what other countries saw as crumbs from the UN table. Just the same, Grenada's entire economy was fueled by three things – tourism, agricultural exports, and international aid. If any of these failed to deliver, the island risked falling into the deadly grip of gangs, drugs, violence, and corruption.

What Val expected from this crowd, once the video ended, were precisely the questions she would have asked. Demanded, really. Starting with, you come to our country, you pay, and then what? If we truly believe this is not a cover for an epidemic of drugs and gangs, we are still facing the threat of our larger neighbors declaring us a pariah. World leaders would be up in arms. What if America and its allies blockade us like they have Cuba?

And so forth.

Instead, what Val observed was the room's occupants became split in two.

The woman and a few others grew increasingly restless. They shifted in what to Val seemed like angry unison. Barely managing to remain present through the video's final minutes.

The others – Val thought the majority of those present – became utterly still. She could not see if they even breathed.

As soon as the screen went blank, before Denton rose and hit the dual switches to turn on the lights and raise the screen, the spokeswoman launched straight in. 'You expect us to believe this?'

Only now the man seated beside her declared, 'I do.'

She was so shocked it took her a moment to swing slowly around. 'You did not just say that.'

'What I just saw, what I read, this is real,' the man replied. 'As real as it gets.'

'I for one am not so gullible.' She stabbed the space between her and Denton. 'This man has a lot to answer for.'

'What more can the gentleman say?'

The woman then realized the room was no longer with her. Val saw it happen. She made a quick scan, and in their faces was an interest, a *hunger*, that shook the spokeswoman to her core.

And not just that one woman.

These dual responses split the two attorneys.

The senior attorney, Rachel Bernstein, was clearly shaken. Her steel-clad distance from the world of clients and courtrooms and legal sparring had been breached. But what troubled Bernstein far more was her young associate's response.

Consuela Almeida's reaction was a vivid declaration, a reaction Val knew all too well.

The draw.

The spokeswoman demanded, 'I have questions and I demand—'

'No!' The man seated next to her thumped the table, startling the woman so that she drew away. He shouted more loudly still, '*No!* This gentleman has said enough. His video is perfectly clear. That and the article are all the evidence I need. Nothing will change your mind. You're against him!'

She showed what to Val looked like genuine fear. 'And you're not?'

'I say we should move on, is what I'm telling you. Didn't you feel it, this thing? He's telling the truth!'

An older gentleman seated directly opposite the pair said, 'You're afraid.'

'Surely, I'm afraid,' the woman replied. 'For my family and my island.'

'So go on being afraid,' the older gentleman said. 'I for one want to ask the next thing.'

'Which is what, exactly?'

He turned to Denton. 'Can I do this?'

'Not just you,' the man seated next to the frightened woman said. He addressed their former spokeswoman. 'Look around you. See what has happened.'

'This is terrible, what you're saying.'

But the older gentleman simply waved her words aside. He asked again, 'Can we join you? You have done this, yes?'

'We all have, the three of us.'

The younger attorney said, 'Me, too. I want in.'

Bernstein tried for outrage, but the tremor in her voice betrayed her. 'This is something the partners need to discuss—'

'Don't stand in my way on this.' Almeida cut off Bernstein's response by getting tight into the senior attorney's face and repeating, '*Don't.*'

The younger man asked, 'You have enough leaves for us all?'

'You're just acting crazy,' the woman seated next to him said. 'All of you.'

Denton replied, 'Since the second tree's destruction, we have been using smaller and smaller portions of the remaining leaves.

What we've discovered is the amount is unimportant. We've begun grinding the leaves into dust. One tiny speck is enough to introduce the desired effect.' He pointed to Connor, as she drew a leather pouch from her purse, opened it, and withdrew a handful of thumbnail-size plastic sleeves. Denton went on, 'Raise your hand, those who want to proceed.'

All but three of those gathered lifted their hands. Including Consuela Almeida, who continued to both silence and challenge Bernstein with her gaze.

As Connor handed around the packets, the spokeswoman moaned, 'Don't do this crazy thing.'

None of those with upraised hands even glanced her way.

Denton accepted a packet and asked, 'Val?'

'Absolutely, yes.'

'In case you are interested, repeating the exercise amplifies aspects of the experience.' He waited while Connor took one for herself and slipped the rest into her purse. 'Just follow our lead.'

SEVEN

Denton remained at the consulate, working with those staff members who were now on their side. Connor walked Val outside to where the SUV idled by the curb. 'You need to get to the airport. I thought you might like some company.'

'Does the companionship come with answers?'

'Some, not a lot,' Connor replied, slipping into the rear seat. 'Which is pretty much all I know.'

As soon as the doors closed, and the driver pulled into traffic, Val asked, 'Where am I going?'

'Bristol by way of Teterboro.'

'The train would be just as fast,' Val protested.

'Bristol, as in England. And to answer your next question, yes, you are traveling by private jet.'

'How much is that costing us?'

'A lot.' Connor smiled. 'First class, baby.'

'All I've got with me is a go-bag filled with dirty clothes.'

Lynda responded from the front passenger seat. 'I've taken the liberty of adding to your wardrobe.'

The driver added, 'This was a major ask. Since my pal Lynda here hates shopping.'

'The sales clerks at Saks made it as painless as possible,' Lynda replied.

'Thanks, I guess.' Val turned to Connor. 'Can I ask why I'm going?'

'Absolutely, you can ask. But all I can tell you is it's part of the same set of instructions out of Canada.' Connor leaned against the side door. 'How did it go with the VP?'

Val glanced at the security. 'Are we safe discussing things?'

'From this point forward, all of the people involved with your movements are on our side.'

'Wow.'

'I know, right? So tell.'

Val gave it to her in succinct bites, mentally shaping the article she would be writing on the flight. When she was done, Connor studied the world beyond the front windscreen, silent. Then, 'I wish I knew where all this was headed.'

'That makes two of us.'

Lynda turned toward Connor and said, 'The pilot requested a call on our approach.'

'Go ahead.' Connor asked Val, 'How is life in Campione?'

'Everyone in my apartment building belongs to our group,' Val replied. 'They've helped as much as anyone can.'

Connor nodded and did the polite thing, pretending to ignore Val's sorrow. 'Andorra was beyond boring. Which helped in a way, the two of us coming to terms with being married. Denton and I are both stubborn and prone to insist we know what's best.' Her smile was canted. 'Not what you'd call a marriage made in heaven. Especially after we lost the ability, you know.'

'To commune.' Val swallowed against the memory. 'Yes. I know.'

'Then Camila Suarez, head of our financial group, contacted us from Monaco. By that point, our funds had grown to where she needed Denton's help with accounting and mine with legal.'

'So,' Val said. 'Monaco.'

'A sunny place full of shady people. When it comes to moving secret money in comfort and style, Monaco is top of the list.' She smiled. 'Speaking of which, your accountant pal Richie Bond is also helping us out. He and Arbila are talking about marriage.'

'I heard.' One of many connections that had been open to her, and still were. If or when she felt like fully rejoining the world.

The traffic congealed as they climbed on to the George Washington Bridge. Val watched a barge trundle down below them, the water sparkling in its passage, and released the thoughts that had plagued far too many nights. 'I keep returning to the same dark suspicion. Bad as a broken record. No matter how I try, it resurfaces. I've come to dread waking up before dawn.'

The car had been silent before. Now the other three seemed to be holding their breath. No one looked her way. Just the same, Val knew they were now on high alert. All of them.

The words remained momentarily choked off, the pressure in her chest rising until she fought for enough air to continue. 'I don't know if it's just loneliness and remorse that drives my early hours dilemma. But it feels like more than that. I push it away, but it keeps coming back. Like it's important I understand. Like Bernard wants me to know.'

The traffic crawled forward. The only sound in their vehicle came from a truck idling in the next lane.

Val said, 'I am becoming increasingly certain Bernard was aware of some danger, some threat. And he saw the only way forward was for him to sacrifice himself.'

Of course, Val was aware that most of their group thought Bernard's death was suspicious. The timing was just too coincidental. And a man of his age and health, dedicated Alpine hiker, never smoked, drank sparingly, brought down by a heart attack? Pu-leese.

Many people in the community – not a majority by any means, but a sizeable proportion – had wanted to cast aside their hidden state and shout their presence to the world. It was time, they declared, to stop hiding. They demanded to become a visible portion of humanity. Bring it all out in the open.

Gradually, against his wishes and Val's better judgment, Bernard had become this group's unofficial spokesperson.

This sentiment, and their numbers, had grown steadily ever since the plane fleeing across the Canadian border had been brought down by the US missile. After that, it was no longer possible to believe or hope the aggressive tactics had ended with the second rowan tree's destruction.

But the majority continued to balk at going public. Taking the fight to their opposition. They continued their endless debate. Once the US government shot down the plane fleeing to Canada, they became more adamant. They issued polite words of caution. Which only further enraged the minority.

So while Bernard had not been alone in his opposition to the council's methods, he had certainly been the most vocal.

Then he died.

Bernard's death was followed almost immediately by their far-flung group losing its ability to mentally join. And suddenly, they had bigger problems. Suspicions regarding Bernard's death were not ignored. Rather, when their group's ability to combine mental forces and inspect on deeper levels was erased, many such issues had to be temporarily set aside. But not forgotten. Not for an instant.

The traffic began moving more swiftly. The driver accelerated, but otherwise no one moved. Val continued, 'It fits into a pattern that otherwise doesn't make sense. How Bernard grew increasingly distant. When I demanded answers, when we fought, all he said was, his experiment and the data had become dangerously skewed. Everything he'd been working toward was threatened. I always assumed he was talking about the lab. Until, you know, he was gone.'

They exited the bridge and slowly worked their way down and around the curlicue leading to the riverside highway.

Val continued, 'I couldn't see how Bernard would let his experiments come between us. Before, he had treated the lab as a sidebar. His favorite way of describing his work in Paris was, a relic. Something from his past that he felt obliged to complete. Other people were still counting on him. People who had done so much to bring him to France, set him up with funding and lab space. All that had taken place before he encountered the rowan. Even so, he owed it to them to complete the research and write it up. But that didn't change how he saw it. A relic from the man and the life's path that no longer fit who he was and where he was going. Those were his exact words.'

Connor began nodding slowly. A gentle rocking, up and down, that was soon followed by Lynda taking up the same motion. Two women who were absorbing what she said. Not so much in agreement as taking it down deep.

Val continued, 'Then he came for that last weekend. I gave him the ultimatum. He had to leave Paris. Either that . . .'

She stopped. Breathed around the pain.

No one spoke. The women continued to nod, their movements almost in tandem.

'Bernard's reaction was beyond confusing. He was resigned. And something more. Almost like . . .'

Connor spoke for the first time. 'Almost like he had been working toward this moment.'

'He told me that I had waited long enough. Too long. Then he left for the station. No bag, not even his briefcase. All his things were still there in the closet, bathroom, wherever. I thought at the time he didn't believe me, that he planned on coming straight back. I had all the arguments ready, the locked front door, the next threat . . .'

'He knew he wasn't going to need them,' Connor said, still nodding. 'It makes perfect sense.'

That was the last anyone said until they pulled up in front of the Teterboro Airport entrance.

Connor rose from the car, waited while Lynda pulled Val's battered go-bag and a new Tumi from the trunk. As the guard entered the private air terminal, Connor said, 'You need to write this up.'

Val waved a vague hand in the direction of where they had come. 'I've got all this new stuff to put down on paper.'

'Val, listen to me.' Connor moved in tight. 'You need to write this *now*. The moment you started talking, this urgency became part of the pressure we're all feeling.' Connor gave that a long moment, then said, 'Call as soon as you know something.'

But Val never found any reason to make that call.

EIGHT

Six thirty the next morning, Kelly was on the narrow drop-down seat in the rear compartment of a kitted-out Cadillac Escalade. Agnes Pendalon, head of the secret investigative unit tasked with eliminating the opposition, was directly across from her, scanning a file. Kelly stared out the side window, the inch-thick glass tinting her view. The sun had risen on a beautiful late September morning. Yet the SUV's interior remained trapped in a bullet-proof gloom. Kelly disliked the narrow fold-down seat. She detested how the SUV compressed the interior air and rendered it tasteless. She hated the waiting. Which happened every time she was summoned to the White House. Her schedule was never her own. She was rendered mute until ordered to speak. She was crammed inside a team and a rhythm dominated by politics and infighting and jockeying for power. Not action. The only positive aspect of her months spent in recovery was that she had been reassigned to her original role as team leader, and shunted back to active duty.

That and how she had been drawn into Vivienne Grace's orbit.

Even when she fundamentally disagreed with the therapist and her directive, Kelly counted herself among the fortunate. These sessions not only offered a chance to emerge from her current dark cave. For the first time since Nathan's murder, she thought there might be a chance of moving on. Enter a future where loss and hollow regret were not a daily burden she carried from the moment she opened her eyes.

But that did not change how she felt about Vivienne's latest verbal knife thrust.

Vivienne was most definitely mistaken about Kelly and her current ops. They faced an enemy they could not clearly identify. They were desperately seeking to stay ahead of the curve, stop the spread, halt this threat to their nation's future.

Just the same, a number of points Vivienne made in her discussion of this new concept, PPD, were right on target.

When she first started these sessions, Kelly left the office trying to throw out Vivienne's pointed observations like a dog shaking off water. No longer. Hard as it was to be stripped bare, which the therapist so often did, these conversations were cleaning out old wounds. The pain might be psychic. No blood flowed. But the results were evident. She was helping Kelly heal. Finally. At long last.

Which was why Kelly gave this new concept such careful consideration.

Multiple instructors at Quantico had repeatedly sounded the warning. Don't become fixated on one particular viewpoint. Stay open to new avenues. Be alert to the unexpected. Keep mind and senses open to potential new risks. Let the evidence speak loud and clear, even if it threatens your case. Accept that your initial suspicions, no matter how well founded they are in logic, could be wrong. A sniper's tight focus will destroy an investigator's ability to solve a case, and eventually end their career.

Kelly did not think this was happening here. She had no idea what alternatives might be present. If any. But that was not the issue.

She was surrounded by people who shared her perspective. She found comfort in listening to those who saw the world and the threat as she did.

The conclusion was clear enough. No matter how disturbing.

She needed to be open to alternative viewpoints. Even if it meant stepping outside her comfort zone.

Then Grey Mathers, Agnes Pendalon's personal aide, interrupted with, 'Incoming.'

Avri Rowe, the president's chief of staff, always traveled by way of a motorcade consisting of three black-on-black armored Escalades. He despised the more standard Tahoes, claimed they were less comfortable than a speedboat pushing through choppy seas. Avri wanted three things from his motorcade: speed, precision, and a deaf ear to everything discussed while underway.

Virtually all conversations between him and Agnes' team took place here. In the middle SUV's rear hold.

This was as close to power central as Kelly Kaiser ever wanted or needed to come.

Avri Rowe emerged from the White House's side entrance with a bulky file under one arm. His other hand held a phone to his ear. He climbed in, dumped his file on the seat between him and Agnes, said no three times. The motorcade was moving before his second denial. Avri then cut the connection, pocketed the phone, opened the file, slipped on his reading glasses, and said, 'Go.'

Kelly liked how Agnes began these discussions with a past event. She couched it so her words sounded like a standard summary briefing, rather than reminding Avri about previous conversations that he might or might not remember. 'Eleven months ago, the French secret service picked up a scientist they identified as a senior member of the opposition. Or rather, they tried to. Bernard Severant was dead of an apparent heart attack when they broke into his lab. At least, that is what they claim. They also failed to inform us of this incident until yesterday. They insist there was no reason to mention it before now, as they did not know he was part of our target group until a routine summary containing his name passed over their supervisor's desk.'

Avri studied Dr Bernard Severant's photograph. Black, handsome, intelligent. Nice smile. 'We're discussing this today because . . .'

'We are fairly certain our telepaths' silence or lack of communication or whatever you want to call it started that very same day.'

Avri turned the page. 'And you're certain this loss of telepathic ability has impacted our opponents as well.'

'We are.'

'So why has this suddenly become a pressing issue?'

'Three items have the potential to explode in our faces. And which might all have originated with this failed arrest.' Agnes pointed her chin at Kelly. Go.

They pulled through the side gates and were saluted by the duty officer as Kelly said, 'Yesterday Valentina Garnier landed at Washington Dulles on an Air France flight, Geneva by way of Paris. Ms Garnier and the deceased Bernard Severant were engaged to be married. We were not alerted to their presence because Ms Garnier traveled under a Grenadian diplomatic passport.'

'What alerted you?'

'After overnighting at an airport hotel, she traveled to the Hay-Adams and met with Carlton Riffkind,' Kelly replied. 'Who also arrived yesterday. From Grenada. Also under a Grenadian passport. We have since learned they have also been appointed official members of Grenada's consular staff to the United Nations.'

'Grenada is still officially a member of the British Commonwealth of Nations,' Agnes said. 'We have heard nothing about all this from our assets in MI6 or their diplomatic corps. Not a peep.'

Kelly continued, 'Yesterday Carlton and Val met Vice President Dale and his daughter in the Hay-Adams' dining room. We had no official notice. The meeting did not make it on to the VP's calendar. We have since learned it was arranged at the last minute by way of Mrs Riffkind and Cynthia Dale. We have no idea what they discussed.'

Rowe growled, 'Schedule a meeting with Terrance Dale.'

'Already in your calendar. Nine this evening. The only time we could arrange at short notice.' She reached over and turned to the file's next page. 'Continue, Kelly.'

'Riffkind and Garnier traveled straight from the Hay-Adams to Union Station. They had lunch in the dead center of the underground food hall. They talked for almost an hour.'

'An echo chamber,' Agnes said. 'No chance of surveillance. We have no idea what they might have discussed—'

'We know,' Avri said.

'Val Garnier traveled alone to New York, where she was joined by a professional security detail. She went straight to the lower Manhattan offices of the law firm Cotton Southerns, where she was joined by Denton Hayes and Connor Breach.'

'Two more names on our red-flag list,' Agnes said. 'Also now holding Grenadian passports.'

The traffic to either side was trapped in silent amber, while their entourage flowed smoothly. Kelly had no idea where they were going and didn't much care. She went on, 'Hayes and Breach have taken an apartment in the Langham. They are accompanied at every step by an attorney from Cotton Southerns and a security team. Val Garnier then flew by private jet to Bristol with a woman we don't recognize.'

'Where?'

'England. Southern Wiltshire,' Agnes said. 'Middle of nowhere. MI5 has been alerted. Whether they'll do anything about this is anyone's guess.'

The trio of SUVs pulled through the Canadian embassy's security gates and halted in the forecourt. Grey Mathers rose from the passenger seat and stood by the rear door, blocking the embassy staffer's approach.

Avri said, 'They're going public.'

Agnes sighed. And with good reason. Her team had spent the past year and a half operating under the radar. No reporters dogging their moves, no congressional hearings, no budgetary oversights. Having the opposition take this step changed everything.

Avri said, 'See if the president can fit us in tomorrow morning. I want you both present for my meeting tonight.' He reached for the door, stopped. 'Four years of searching and we still don't have anything on Dale?'

'His daughter,' Agnes offered.

Avri shook his head. 'She's been clean, what, a year?'

'Longer.'

'Won't wash.' Avri glared at the embassy, so intent he might as well have been searching for a way to breach the structure. 'So you know, the office of Canada's prime minister is demanding a public apology. They insist that it come from the president himself. Otherwise, they will try our team in military court and televise it.' Avri opened his door. 'Find me something on Dale. If you can't, invent something.'

NINE

The vice president's residence was located at the United States Naval Observatory. Completed in 1893, it stood on the crest of a low hill and was surrounded by eighty wooded acres, multiple fences, and around-the-clock security. The result was a rare gift of seclusion and privacy. This time of year, the Dale family often ate on the rear patio. The faint whisper of distant traffic only added to the sense of isolation.

Following the second rowan tree's destruction a year and a half earlier, Carlton and his wife had sheltered in the vice president's residence for almost a month. Carlton knew by way of his previous stay that, whenever possible, Terrance Dale followed a very precise routine. He tried to return home by seven in the evening to have dinner with his family. This happened far more often than with the president or the inner circle, where Dale was most definitely not welcome.

Straight upon arriving, Terrance handed the briefcase and phone to his security. He rounded the side of their home, entered the pool house, donned a bathing suit and swam a fast half-mile. He showered in the pool house and dressed in casual clothes. Only then did he enter their home.

Terrance Dale's wife, Cynthia, still taught graduate-level classes in art history and restoration at Georgetown. She was also an excellent chef and enjoyed cooking for the family when time permitted. Tonight, she had their meal set in chafing dishes by the patio table when Terrance appeared. He greeted Carlton with, 'You're here. Good.'

Cynthia kissed her husband, said, 'Carlton is here for the duration.'

'So am I, Daddy,' Lauren said. 'That is, assuming you commit.'

'That defines Terrance's entire life and world,' Cynthia replied. 'Committed.'

'He knows what I mean, and so do you.'

Terrance gave no sign he heard. He told Carlton, 'I'm glad you're here.'

That was the last any of them spoke of the pending events until dinner was finished and coffee served. At that point, Terrance's motions took on a formal precision. Lining his cup and spoon. Refusing Cynthia's offer of dessert with a solemn thanks. Waiting until the table was still and silent. Then, 'This afternoon, I decided an official gesture was required. Call it an offer of conciliation, if you will. Because that was what I hoped to receive. The president would hear from me, the outsider, that their unofficial and highly secret directive was not working. In fact, it endangered us as a nation. We were potentially more threatened by what they were intending than by the alternative'.

'Outstanding,' Lauren said. When her mother turned and glared, Lauren demanded, 'What?'

'There have been many wonderful changes to your life and character since taking that first step,' Cynthia told her daughter. 'But you still have difficulty knowing when you need to refrain from speaking. So I'm telling you, with all the love at my disposal, now is the time to zip it.'

Terrance ignored the exchange. 'I went personally to the president's secretary and requested five minutes. I didn't ask for privacy because I knew it wouldn't happen. The secretary fit me in at half past four, which is an astonishment. I assume she found me the slot because it was the first time I'd ever made such a request.'

Terrance paused to drink from his cup, then scanned the night sky. Lightning bugs flitted around the back garden and across the pool's surface. Night birds chirped from the surrounding glade. A horn blared far in the distance. They waited.

'Most of us are defined by one element above all else. First and foremost, it's what we do. Our professional calling. Our purpose in life. Whatever you want to call it. This is our primary defining trait.' A pause, then, 'As I stood there in the president's outer office, I realized this had been missing from my life. For at least a year now. The president and his senior staff were headed in one direction. And I refused to follow their lead. Which had left me adrift. I felt ashamed it had taken me this long to realize what was happening.'

Cynthia reached over and took hold of the hand resting on the table. Terrance looked down at the fingers now intertwined with his. Finally, 'There were seven others in the Oval Office. Avri was at the Canadian embassy, which actually helped on several levels. His senior staffer and four military were there, plus the secretary . . .' He lifted his free hand and gave a vague wave. Not important. 'I used the Canadian situation as the reason for my urgency. I pointed out that our expeditionary force was in breach of treaties that date back to our country's early history. I urged the president to formally disengage from their pursuit of these so-called enemies of the state. The risk to his re-election was huge. He needed deniability. He needed to decry the invasion as something that happened without his direct knowledge or involvement. Offer Canada the formal apology they were demanding. Refuse to take the course being laid out by certain members of his cabinet. At least until after the election.'

Then he went silent.

Finally, Carlton asked, 'His response?'

'The president said he would give my suggestions careful consideration. I thanked him and left.' Terrance looked at Carlton. 'I won't take such a monumental step as some vague act of defiance. No matter how vehemently I disagree with their current policy.'

Lauren said, 'Daddy, please. There's nothing vague about their reprisals—'

Cynthia broke in, 'Daughter.'

'Mom, really? You especially—'

'When it's time for you to speak again, I'll be sure and let you know.' To her husband, 'Go on, dear.'

'No series of acts in support of one single policy justifies such a step as what you're asking me to take. No matter how reprehensible.'

Cynthia said, 'I agree.'

Lauren's mouth dropped open. Aghast. But silent.

'The issue is one of overall direction. I fundamentally disapprove of the course they are setting for this nation.'

'And doing so in secret,' Cynthia added.

'Exactly. There must be a public reckoning. I will not stand by and allow them to class these fine citizens as enemies of the state. Or declare some of our nation's closest allies to be pariahs. Because of this.'

Cynthia repeated, 'In secret.'

'Of course in secret. How else could they make such an idiotic move?' He addressed Carlton, 'If the president ignores my appeal, I will agree to your request, take this step, on one condition. This is to be a real campaign. I've no intention to simply put myself forward as a sacrificial—'

Cynthia said sharply, 'Don't you dare finish that sentence.' When she was certain her husband was remaining silent, she asked Carlton, 'Perhaps I should already know this. But have you ever run a national campaign?'

'Twice,' Carlton replied. 'They both lost.'

'So. A perfect record.' To Lauren, 'Thank you very much, dear. I know it cost you.'

'I have a hundred questions and a thousand comments,' Lauren said. 'Just one can't wait. I want in.'

'And I wouldn't have it any other way.' Terrance glanced at his watch and rose from the table. 'Thank you for the lovely meal. I need to change. I'm due back at the White House. Carlton, be so kind as to join me for the drive.'

TEN

The meeting with the Canadian ambassador had left Avri Rowe in a foul mood.

They gathered in the conference room adjacent to Rowe's White House office. He had another office on the OEOB's second floor, where his staff was located. This one was much smaller, but it was just down the corridor from the Oval Office. The conference room was officially open to all senior staff. But early in the term, Rowe had staked claim. It was exclusively his in all but name.

What made Rowe's mood so much worse was news of Dale's meeting with the president. Agnes Pendalon was clearly concerned about Avri possibly demolishing an already bruised relationship. 'Your senior staffer was in the meeting. Dale simply—'

'He went behind my back.' Avri's bark held an acidic edge. One notch off full-blown rage. 'He arranged the meeting for when I was tied up with that Canadian ponce.'

'You don't know that.' Agnes held a printout from the president's daily timesheet. 'He asked for an urgent meeting. He did not specify the time. He was given the only slot available.'

Avri smoldered.

'We already know he is not in favor of our approach to hunt down those who have encountered the rowan and its leaves—'

Avri growled. 'He's come out for the enemy.'

'He expressed his concerns. Which, you have to admit, holds water.'

His glare now had a direction. 'I can't believe you said that.'

Kelly spoke for the first time since entering the conference room. 'Actually, sir, Agnes has made a point we need to consider seriously.'

Avri's gun-barrel gaze swiveled in her direction.

Kelly went on, 'There is a very real possibility the Canadian government's demand for a presidential apology means our entire game plan is going to be forced into the open.'

'Who we are, why we're operating as we do, what alliances we've built up,' Agnes said. 'We risk everything being revealed.'

Kelly continued, 'Dale offered the president an option that makes a lot of sense.'

'We know the vice president has been against us from the start,' Agnes said.

'He's never said anything in that regard,' Avri retorted. 'Not once.'

'He doesn't need to,' Agnes replied. 'Given the fact that his only daughter and perhaps his wife are counted among the enemy. Who knows, perhaps the vice president has taken that step as well.'

There it was again. The second time that day that Agnes Pendalon had applied the word *enemy*. Kelly did not disagree. Far from it. Just the same, it brought up all the questions, all the challenges her therapist had posed.

When Avri remained silent, Agnes told her, 'Finish your thought.'

Kelly said, 'Tonight's meeting is our only opportunity to prepare for what may already be coming down the line. Because if we are faced with public exposure, Dale's attitude is suddenly going to be the preferred option for a lot of the American public.'

Avri did not respond.

'We need to know what he and Carlton Riffkind and Val Garnier discussed. Did this meeting have some connection to the official tie they've established with Grenada? Why has this group suddenly appeared in Washington and New York? And why now? Why are they exposing themselves to arrest?'

Avri Rowe kept quiet.

Kelly continued, 'The president has informed you he is not going to do as Dale requested. We need to know Dale's next step. What will he do when he learns there will be no apology?'

Avri continued to study Kelly in silence until there was a tap on the door. 'Come.'

A staffer stepped inside. 'Sir, Vice President Dale has arrived.'

* * *

Despite her personal feelings about the man, Kelly had to admit Terrance Dale looked every inch the senior statesman. Presidential, in fact. A strong and virile man, weathered by multiple storms, bearing the weight of years with grace. Dale entered the conference room and seated himself and waited.

'Mister Vice President.'

'Avri.'

'Thank you for meeting with us. Sorry about the hour.'

Dale was dressed in navy slacks, dress shirt, V-neck sweater. Yet somehow on him it looked formal. He was seated across from Avri, with Agnes and Kelly lined up at the conference table's far end. The table itself was bare, save for the speaker phone poised like a miniature launch vehicle at its center. The light blinked green, indicating that General Skarren had joined them. The vice president gave no sign he even noticed the invisible listener.

The president's chief of staff cleared his throat. Then asked, 'We were wondering if you could tell us what you and Carlton Riffkind discussed.'

'Most certainly. It's a valid question. Would you happen to know what response the president has to my suggestion?'

'He has given your words his most serious consideration.'

Dale simply waited.

'Unfortunately, he has opted not to follow your proposed course of action.'

The vice president winced. This was not some theatrical reaction. Kelly could see Rowe's response caused him very real pain.

Dale breathed out through pursed lips. Stared at nothing. Breathed again.

'Mr Vice President—'

'Carlton has asked me to run for president in the upcoming November elections.'

The room froze solid. The speakerphone gave off a soft grunt, as if Skarren had been gut shot.

Dale glanced at the apparatus, then turned back to Avri and said, 'He wants me to run as an independent.'

Avri's cough carried the soft punch of a silenced pistol.

Dale went on, 'There is a precedent. Thomas Jefferson was

vice president when he ran against incumbent President John Adams in 1800. Of course, that was before the current "ticket" system was in place, whereby the VP is in the same party—'

'This is insane.'

Dale continued, 'Were I to agree, obviously, I would resign from the party. It would be up to the president whether I should also step down from my role—'

'You can *not* be serious.' Rowe's features appeared parboiled. 'Why would you even *consider* such an idiotic gesture?'

Terrance Dale swept his arm in a semi-circle, taking in the room, the three of them, the silent speaker phone. 'You know perfectly well why.'

'You'd risk handing our opponents the White House?'

'Not,' Terrance calmly replied, 'if I win.'

'Ridiculous! You don't have anywhere near enough time to make the filing deadlines in all fifty states! Much less prepare a national campaign!'

'Carlton assures me all this has been taken care of,' Terrance responded. 'I happen to believe him.'

Avri's features appeared to balloon with the effort required not to leap across the table and throttle him. 'All your looney pals must be thrilled with your dive off the deep end.'

Terrance did not respond.

His silence only added fuel to Avri's rage. '*You are joining the enemy.*'

Terrance met his gaze with a stoic calm.

'You'll become the nation's worst traitor since Alger Hiss!'

Terrance rose to his feet. 'I will inform the president of my decision well in advance of any public announcement.'

When he left the room, Avri growled, 'I've despised that turncoat since day one.'

No one spoke.

He jerked to his feet, shooting his chair back so hard it hammered the side wall. 'Arrest them.' He stalked to the door. 'Arrest them all.'

Agnes waited until the door slammed shut. Then, 'General?'

'This is terrible news.'

Agnes nodded agreement, but merely said, 'What Avri just

ordered. The arrests. Carlton Riffkind is residing at the VP's home.'

Kelly added, 'The others who are out in the open – Denton Hayes, Valentina Garnier, and Connor Breach – are now represented by one of New York's top firms of litigators.'

'Connor Breach was also formerly clerk to a Supreme Court justice,' Agnes added.

'Their arrest would mean a courtroom brawl,' Kelly said. 'We'd be forced to show our hand. Probably in federal court.'

'Which may be their aim all along,' Agnes said. 'A legal battle timed to Dale announcing—'

Skarren broke in with, 'I am formally countermanding Rowe's order.'

Agnes leaned back, spent. 'Thank you, General.'

'Give me a day. I'll set up a face-to-face with Avri once he's had a chance to cool down. Lay it all out. He'll come around.'

'I sincerely hope so, sir.'

'Monitor, observe, prepare,' Skarren replied. 'The outcomes of most battles are decided before the first shot is fired.'

ELEVEN

Val spent the transatlantic flight following Connor's advice. She did her best to work through all the tumult and fret and hollow worries and pain surrounding Bernard's death. Val started with a vague hope that the act of forming an article might prove cathartic. Drain away some of the burden she carried. Instead, she gradually became filled with the same sense of growing intensity that Connor had described.

By the time their plane landed in Bristol, there was little space left in Val's interior world for anything except what was coming next. Whatever that might be.

As they passed through customs, a text message pinged on Lynda's phone. The instructions from Canada were exactly as Carlton had described, terse to the point of rudeness. *Hire a car. Drive to Marlborough. Rest. Be ready.*

Their hotel on the outskirts of Marlborough had one suite, which they took. Lynda insisted on taking the parlor's fold-out sofa.

Val's final dream returned her to that dark and silent realm. One filled with beings that made it all seem not just right but good. She was welcomed into a world where she could neither see nor speak, and yet which was beautiful in a manner she could not understand. The dreamtime experience lasted a single breath. Less. Then she awoke with a gasp, leaped from bed, and stood by the open window, watching the sunrise and waiting for her heart rate to slow.

She entered the suite's parlor to find Lynda already dressed and ready for the day. She greeted Val with the news that their Canadian contacts remained silent. Ditto when the two women checked their emails. So they relaxed and enjoyed a massive English breakfast. Fried eggs, huge British-style sausage links, what the waitress called a rasher of bacon but looked like two hand-size slabs of fried ham, baked beans, hash browns, black pudding, toast and marmalade for dessert. They ate until their stomachs groaned. Like they had been on a starvation diet for weeks.

They returned to their room and stretched out and laughed over a meal that left them dazed. Ninety minutes later, they were alerted by Lynda's phone chiming with an incoming message. The text held just six letters and numbers, which Lynda explained was a British-style postcode. She went online and said it was for a parking lot in the town of Avebury, just six miles away. They were not due to arrive for almost an hour and a half, so after checking out, they stopped for a coffee. A double expresso later, Val thought she was fairly ready for whatever came next.

It was far from the first time that life had proven her wrong.

Their Hertz rental was a Volvo SUV. The ride was quiet, smooth, and zippy whenever the road opened up. The highway followed an illogical path, weaving around some hills, climbing others. They passed through three villages, and each time the road narrowed rather than widened, trapping them in slow-moving commercial traffic. Then they entered the countryside, the sun shone on emerald fields, and their slow progress no longer mattered.

They passed a sign declaring Avebury to be a UNESCO World Heritage Site, rounded a corner, and on their right rose the oddest hill Val had ever seen. The base was a nearly perfect circle, rising steeply to a grassy crown. Its actual size could only be judged by the ant-sized people on its slopes.

Lynda said, 'Silbury Hill.'

'What is it?'

'Nobody knows. For years, they thought it was a prehistoric burial site. But decades of searching haven't uncovered any hint of bones or artifacts.'

Most of the hikers held to well-worn tracks that spiraled gradually upwards. The few who made a straight-line ascent used the tall grass for hand-holds. 'You mean it's man-made?'

'I mean no one knows. Archaeologists claim it dates to around seven thousand years ago.'

'Spooky.'

'Spooky works as well as anything, I suppose.' Lynda pointed at the way ahead. 'I came here a few times as a child. You've heard of Stonehenge, right?'

'Of course.'

'The Avebury stones are much older. Estimates are between two and three thousand years before Stonehenge. But this place isn't some orderly circle of pillars, and the stones themselves aren't nearly so impressive. Which is why most tourist buses go to the other place. Standing stones, they're called nowadays. They stretch out over a couple of miles, two arms that might have once marked processional ways leading to a pair of concentric circles lined on one side by the village and the other by a great earthen dike. The circles and the pathways are all missing stones, and the ruddy dike's so large it's easy to mistake it for just another weird part of a very strange landscape . . .'

Val wasn't sure whether Lynda stopped talking, or if she suddenly lost the ability to hear. There was simply no room for anything other than the change.

It had probably been building for some time. But it was only when Lynda took the turning toward Avebury village that she realized . . .

Val asked, 'You feel that?'

Lynda nodded a second time. 'Like you said. Spooky.'

Intensity.

But other words came to mind almost as fast. Ones she had not applied to herself in almost two years.

The draw.

For one brief instant, Val was swept back to where it all began, that first night in the Russian glade, there in the heart of the Kuril Islands. A nowhere place on Russia's eastern coast. Val had remained just outside the circle of crystal trees. Watching as everyone in the group save her walked toward the illuminated rowan tree. Accepted the leaf that became a spiral of light, and absorbed it into their bodies. Becoming illuminated themselves. And far more besides.

This was much more than a memory. She was there. Reliving from the inside.

Val transitioned to that moment when she finally accepted the rowan's invitation. She had been seated in her living room, and beside her was the man that was no more. The man who, for a too-brief period, made Val feel complete. Bernard guided her through taking the leaf she had carried with her since Kuril. Talking softly, keeping her anchored as she watched the leaf become something else, breathing it in, and beginning the course that brought her to this moment.

The draw.

Val breathed in and out, struggling to fit the old sensation into this new situation. She asked Lynda, 'You OK?'

Their vehicle crawled forward, scarcely above a walking pace. Lynda shuddered like a dog shaking off rain. 'Define OK.'

The road was narrow and the traffic heavy. To their left stretched a gently sloping meadow that paralleled the road into Avebury. Two lines of stones marched up the grassy expanse. Val did not need anyone to tell her these rocks were old. Their shapes were oddly divergent, as if the era when they were created did not value symmetry. They were mostly twice her height, planted in the meadow as if they had been expected to take root and grow. They formed parallel rows about forty feet apart. Cows grazed calmly as tourists walked the green expanse.

Lynda followed the sat nav's instructions and drove around the village's central traffic circle. She entered a narrow lane, then turned into a parking area marked by multiple signs saying the spaces were reserved for local residents and disabled only.

The corner space was taken by a Mercedes minibus. The door opened, giving a glimpse of the passengers inside, and a strikingly handsome man in his early to mid-fifties stepped out and pointed to the next space. When Lynda parked and cut her motor, the man opened the rear door, slipped inside, and offered them a blue plastic envelope. 'Set that on your dash so the local parking guards don't have you towed. You're Val, right? I'm Sean Stiles.'

'Hi. This is Lynda.'

He pointed to the bus. 'Greg Alderton needs you to come play observer.'

'And Greg is . . .'

'He serves as de facto head of the Canadian faction. Greg

would also tell you there's about a dozen things wrong in what I just said.' Sean pointed to a pale young man stepping from the minibus. 'Here he comes now.'

The instant Greg appeared, Val sensed a vivid connection. Which was beyond strange.

Eleven months back, on approaching a stranger, Val could reach out and bond. But only if the other was open and intent and willing.

Since the breakdown or whatever it was, though, nothing.

Greg walked in the disjointed manner of someone coming to terms with unfamiliar limbs. He lifted each leg carefully and set his foot into place. As though he was relearning how to walk. Just the same, he moved fast.

Greg's first words were, 'We've got exactly forty-seven minutes to do this and flee the scene.'

Sean's voice took on the singsong tone of a parent teaching a young child. 'Good morning, Val. Hello, Lynda. I'm Greg. So nice to meet you both.'

But the pale young man was already moving. 'Sean thinks if he repeats polite words often enough, I'll change. Maybe someday. Right now, we don't have time. OK if we hurry?'

'I guess,' Val said, falling into step beside him. 'Do you feel this – I'm not sure what to call it.'

'Oh, yeah. Definitely.'

'What is it?'

'No idea. Nice, though. Right?'

They joined a tourist group following a guide with a little flag tied to her sealed umbrella. Val asked, 'Is this experience something you regularly have in Canada?'

'I wish.' He began threading his way forward. 'We need to pick up the pace.'

'Where are we going?'

He pointed in the vague direction of a circle of stones. 'Over there.'

'Can I ask why?'

'Absolutely. And the answer is, I have no idea.'

They crossed the street, passed through a wooden gate, and

entered a field holding the largest stones of all. The earthen dike rose to her right, a long steep-sided hill that merged with the meadow. To her left was the village church, town hall, stores. Tourists walked the dike's crest, wandered around the field, tromped off into the distance. These standing stones formed a pair of vague circles, one inside the other. Greg said, 'Working on these transition points has been incredibly difficult. With the investments, it's all crystal clear. We get moments when all our synapses fire in tandem. So we send off very specific instructions. Buy, sell, whatever. But with this, it's been tight little bursts. Do this, go there, be ready.' He entered a vast open space surrounded by the irregular stones. 'And in your case, the instructions were to bring an official observer.'

'Thanks. I'm glad you decided on me. This has already been great.'

'It wasn't like that at all.' Greg halted in what might have been the center of the inner circle and checked his watch. 'You being here was the clearest burst of all. It had to be you.'

'I'm honored, I guess.' She pointed behind them, back to the parking area. 'What about the others who came with you?'

'None of them move easy. And we've got to be somewhere else very soon. They have to be there for that.'

'You mean, something beyond our standing here in the middle of nowhere?'

'I know. Wild, right?' Greg checked his watch once more. 'Ninety seconds.'

Then it struck her. 'This may sound totally weird.'

Greg scanned the horizon, searching. 'More than standing here waiting for whatever comes next?'

'Do you ever have these dreams of, I actually don't know how . . .What?'

He was watching her now. Intense. Focused. 'The black that's beautiful. People who aren't. You know. Aren't people.'

Val breathed, managed, 'Woah.'

He straightened, sniffed the air, whispered, 'I think it's happening.'

TWELVE

Val found it mildly amazing how the hikers and tourists and families continued swirling around them, oblivious to how she and Greg stood at the eye of a hurricane.

The swirling mass of energy coalesced. Tighter and tighter. Focused upon the point where they stood.

Val decided a storm this potent needed a name. Even if it remained a secret she never shared.

Greg said, 'Five seconds.'

Val whispered the storm's name. Bringing her beloved into the moment. As it should be.

Bernard.

WHOOM.

When Val first bonded with the rowan leaf, the resulting experience was so gentle it could easily have gone unnoticed. Val had remained seated on her living-room sofa, Bernard there beside her, smiling, patient, happy. Gradually, gently, the others had reached out in greeting.

This event was something else entirely.

The storm passed. But not the experience.

The after-effect brought to Val's mind the expanding blast zone following a nuclear explosion. She could actually sense the power reaching out *globally.*

And yet all around her people continued walking, cycling, playing with children . . .

Only not all of them.

A few people within visual range, not many, became frozen in place. They focused intently on where the two of them stood. Val watched four women stumble down from the dike's walking path and rush toward them on unsteady legs. They were joined by a family of six, threading their way through the outer circle of stones. A few others followed, all sharing an expression of eager astonishment.

Greg said, 'We have to go.'

She felt it too. The searing urgency to enter into a new phase. Val pointed at a clutch of six backpackers now heading their way and asked, 'What about them?'

He was already moving. 'You know the answer to that.'

And she did. Regardless of how far this next phase took her, they would all be in it together.

The bond was restored.

Greg began running. 'Val, we have to go *now*.'

Neither she nor Lynda spoke during the forty-minute drive. Val considered the car's silence an important opportunity to digest what had just happened. Which on one level was beyond strange. In the lonely weeks following Bernard's death, cut off from communicating with all remaining members of her group, silence became Val's enemy. The quiet hour was something she fought against.

During those lonely months, Val dove headfirst into fusion jazz. It needed to be a totally new sound, a musical dimension completely removed from her past.

Val became desperately involved in studying artists and their development. She grew familiar with how trends shaped and changed over time. On the hardest nights, David Sanborn wept with her. When faced with another bleak morning, Jesse Cook's flamenco-laced jazz got her engine started.

Daytime hours, Val pushed hard on a new writing project, a book relating events that would hopefully someday come to light.

Then, two months ago, Denton Hayes reached out. He asked her to move to Zurich and work with a professional film editor and a sound engineer, putting together their new video. The twelve-hour days, the new city, the joining in a new project with others in their group, granted Val the first hint that her dark hour might finally, at long last, be coming to an end.

Today's silence, as they followed the minibus up the winding countryside lane, could not have been any more different.

Every moment, every breath was filled with new significance. So many past events were being forged together. She could not explain how this was happening, much less why. Just the same, the aura of monumental flow left her able to view her experiences and even her loss as part of a greater whole. Val knew it might all be momentary, a mere side effect resulting from the jolt she'd had in the stone circle. She was almost OK with that. Because for this one brief instant, it was so very good to think her dreadful period was coming to a close.

Up and up they went, the road bound on both sides by emerald meadows and hundreds upon hundreds of sheep. And still they climbed.

As they approached the crest, Val saw it resembled a spine more than a hill, running in both directions as far as she could see.

'The Ridgeway was used by travelers since prehistoric times.' Lynda pointed to her left. 'Beyond Marlborough are burial grounds over ten thousand years old.'

Val heard the words because Lynda actually spoke them. But she found the silent component carried a far greater impact. Because of what the unspoken represented.

Throughout their journey, they had been joined by others. Val was making mental notes now, preparing what she knew would become the key element of a new article, possibly an entire book. A crucial question was whether they had all been present since the stone circle. She thought it was perhaps the case, but could not be certain. Just the same, that was what she suspected had happened. Only now these people were gradually becoming aware of the linkage, and thus able to share their journey.

Lynda spoke slowly, carefully enunciating each word. She also took a soft pause following every phrase. She talked about an era before the Romans came to England. How this narrow ridge granted travelers a unique protection from marauders, because the steep treeless slopes offered few places for bandits to hide and then pounce.

Val thought the way Lynda spoke, breathing around the enormity of what they were doing, confirmed her suspicions. To Val's mind, Lynda's unsteady explanation was precisely how it might sound if the woman was relearning to communicate with these unseen people.

They crested the rise, and a stunning vista opened up in front of them. The view was shared by thousands of silent companions. More. All of them absorbing the sight, Lynda's words, and far more besides. All of them revisiting the same nearly forgotten lessons. Reveling in connecting. But not like before. This was something entirely different. Something far more intense.

Added to this was a growing awareness of an event waiting just up ahead. What that might be, Val had no idea.

'The Pewsey Vale,' Lynda said, starting their descent. 'Archaeologists think this was where the first prehistoric communities in England were established.'

For the first time in eleven months, Val was fully engaged in the moment. She belonged here. The sheer intensity of *now* filled her senses.

And she was not alone in feeling this way.

They were all there in the moment together. Val found herself able to shift her awareness and draw old friends into focus. Connor and Denton in New York. Jared and Laura in DC. Arbila and Richie in Monaco. Friends and contacts lost to her eleven-month fog.

A second set of hills rose perhaps ten miles further south. Between them extended a broad swath of flatland. A glistening ribbon of water ran along its heart. Autumn sun rested gentle on the land, illuminating orderly fields and quiet villages and . . .

They rounded a tight bend in the road, and both women gasped in unison.

And not just them. From all sides came a chorus of astonishment as the multitude of distant observers realized they had arrived.

THIRTEEN

Over the years, Val had seen numerous photographs of crop circles. The designs held a unique mystery, artwork that made no sense. Perfectly symmetrical shapes laid out in fields of corn or soy or wheat or sunflowers. Farmers hated them, because they often resulted in hordes of tourists and UFO seekers mangling their fields. It had become the standard response to a new crop circle for the farmer to cut the entire field the very instant one appeared.

From their position, a few hundred feet above the valley floor, the design was a series of interlinked quarter moons. They spun in three tight arms, like a sea creature whose limbs flowed according to unseen currents. A perfect circle perhaps fifty feet wide formed the pattern's center. They reached the valley road and drove the half-mile to where a county sign marked a parking area for hikers. A narrow trail ran between two fields and then climbed the ridgeline. High up near the hill's crest, a running horse over fifty meters long had been carved into the pale stone.

They parked behind the minibus, almost filling the narrow parking area. A rusting blue sign read *White Horse Trail Walkers Layby*, which she found oddly charming. Val opened her door and straightened slowly. The windless afternoon was filled with the fragrances of autumn. The air quivered with everything that was about to unfold. Val knew she would remember this moment for the rest of her life, and how a polite British sign was enough to make her smile. It might as well have read *Stop Here For Emotional Resuscitation.*

Unloading the minibus required about ten minutes. Val and Lynda helped ready the wheelchairs and walkers. Most of the passengers moved under their own steam, but at a relatively slow pace. Three had to be pushed in chairs. Val took one, Lynda and Sean the others.

The uneven path soon had Val breathing hard. Val's chair belonged to a smiling middle-aged woman who introduced herself as Theresa. Sean pushed an overly still and lumpish young man who did not speak. Lynda's chair held an elderly woman who hummed an occasional solitary note.

Val did not mind the slow going. Not at all. The connection to all those unseen others continued to build, such that the previous eleven months might never have existed. In one sense, they had already arrived at their destination. Regardless of what happened once they reached the crop circle, she was precisely settled into the heart of this new event. Beyond glad they had selected her as the professional witness, having a role to play in this slow procession.

Greg fell into step just as Val's thoughts congealed into two sets of questions. The first had to do with the immediate process they were experiencing.

The second was, 'Tell me about these messages you've been getting.'

'They carried the same sort of force as what we're feeling now,' Greg said. 'That is, assuming your world has just been severely rocked.'

'These messages never lasted very long.' Theresa, the woman in Val's wheelchair, spoke for the first time. 'Afterwards, so many of our group engaged in endless conversations. So very boring. I always took my knitting and headphones. The ones that stop sounds.'

'Noise canceling,' Sean offered.

'Which precisely sums up those meetings,' Theresa said. 'Every now and then, I'd lift one earpiece. Five seconds of that noise, then back I'd go to Beethoven.'

'I always saw those moments when we reconnected as cracks in the wall,' Sean offered.

'A blinding sliver of awareness,' Greg said, nodding. 'Ten seconds later, poof. Gone.'

'Less than ten seconds,' Theresa said. 'Not even close to that long.'

'Ten, five, one,' Greg said. 'Time was never the issue until after.'

'Whoosh and gone,' Sean agreed.

'You know how a lightning flash can blind you?' Theresa said. 'That's how it felt afterwards.'

'Those flashes of insight were so important,' Greg said. 'The messages we received were secondary in a way. We lived for those chances to reconnect.'

Theresa craned her neck to look at Val. 'How ever did you manage without them?'

'It was very hard,' Val conceded. She asked Greg, 'Are you reading my thoughts?'

It was a valid question. Previously, no one easily communicated in words. Doing so required a different sort of link, an open and intense harmony that few managed, and rarely for very long. With most people, it was like trying to communicate during an electrical storm. The static was so intense it felt almost painful to even try. A tight-knit group unified by a single-minded purpose shared snatches of words and images. But this happened almost involuntarily, at moments when they were focused on a joint goal. Val had often felt such wordless bonds with Bernard, especially in their most intimate moments. Words were the medium of her day job, her profession. In joining with her beloved, she wanted to move *beyond* words.

'No,' Greg replied. 'That hasn't changed. But we've been having these moments of communing . . .' Greg smiled at her. 'They're our signal of another incoming explosion.'

'Incoming isn't how I think these happen,' Sean said. 'They don't arrive from somewhere beyond us. I think it's more like grinding a hand generator. Our limited powers of connection build until it's intense enough to create the spark.'

Greg and Theresa and Lynda were all studying him now. Greg said, 'That actually makes sense. Sort of.'

Theresa laughed out loud.

'Anyway, one minute we're just this group of stragglers. Then all of a sudden we start walking together—'

'Those of us who can walk,' Theresa said.

'Moving in tight unison. *Thinking* together. All part of this momentary flow. Then . . .' Sean grinned a second time. 'Like I said. Boom.'

'Then we go back to being stragglers again,' Theresa said.

Sean was the first to stop. He lifted his face to the sky. Squinted. Said, 'Something's wrong.'

Val felt it then. Entering into this moment was a team in pursuit. They were here because they hunted. Their intentions, their focus, everything about their presence was *wrong*.

The others sensed it as well. All of them halted in their tracks. Frozen in place. Staring at the unseen.

Sean said, 'It's them, all right. The group who want to destroy us.'

One of the others fretted, 'Maybe we should abort?'

Theresa shifted in her chair, like she wanted desperately to stand. 'We can't.'

'We need to be there precisely on time,' Greg said.

'Hang on.' Theresa's head swiveled. Searching. 'I feel . . .'

'What?'

She revealed an impish smile. 'We can shut the door.'

Soon as Val heard, she knew it was possible. 'I agree.'

'So do I,' Lynda said. 'Close them out. Seal the telepathic portal.'

'Works for me,' Val said.

'On my three,' Theresa said. 'One, two . . .'

It was as simple as slamming and locking a door. Simpler. More like, they joined together in a unified effort and, click, the others were excluded.

Those hunters, the top-secret team who considered Val's group to be the enemy . . .

All of them. Gone.

Val had never worked on a combat story. But several of her articles and the book that won her the Pulitzer had brought her into intimate contact with soldiers in the field. They often used the term, surgical strike, both in jokes and referring to past missions. Taking out the enemy, shielding civilians, no one except the bad guys entering their crosshairs.

Shutting out these telepaths who wanted to do them harm carried an almost frightening intensity. The force they had mustered was made even more astonishing by how easy this had been. How swift the act. Plus there was the unquestionable fact they all now faced.

They were changing. One incredible event piled upon the next.

The group clustered on the trail stood in silence, trying to come to terms with what they had just done. What it meant. Where their new boundaries might now reach.

Greg said, 'We need to hurry.'

FOURTEEN

Carlton worked from dawn until late morning, only leaving his bedroom office to recharge his mug. The messages he was receiving, both from Denton and those coming from his wife and daughter, all pointed to one essential theme: every minute counted. Every second.

His sat phone calls and Zoom connections forged a steady flow of preparatory steps. His aim was to have the entire campaign team prepped and positioned for the starting gun, if indeed Terrance Dale decided to step in front of the global press and announce his intention to run for the presidency after letting the president know his intentions.

Several times that morning, Carlton was halted by the question of whether he should inform his friend where the guidance originated. Who had actually suggested the vice president leave his party and forge a new path. How it came from a group of individuals who would have previously been considered physically disabled and some as having learning disabilities. This collective resided four hundred miles from the nearest paved road. And they now had a small splinter group stationed in the middle of an English crop circle.

No, the vice president probably didn't need to hear about that just yet.

Nine forty-five found Carlton standing by the kitchen window finishing a plate of over-cooked eggs. He had a dozen semi-urgent matters that needed doing. Even so, he was held in place by two things. The first was a text from his wife, sent via a bank in Singapore where the group held numerous accounts. It was the standard cut-out, which people who knew about such things insisted was both necessary and growing more important with every passing day. The text included a dark web portal address and half the required password for a video conference call. And a time.

Eight minutes.

His second reason for remaining where he was stood thirty feet away. Lauren Dale, the vice president's daughter, was a force of nature. Never still. Rarely able to keep herself in one place long enough to conclude a meal or a chat. Yet there she stood, planted in the center of the rear lawn, staring at the surrounding forest of oak and pine and maple, as immobile as the statuary beyond the pool house. Carlton saw the lone guard on duty step into view for the third time, checking on Lauren.

Which was when his phone rang. The readout said it was the VP's private phone. Just the same, Carlton was tempted to let it go to voice mail. He connected and said, 'Terrance, sorry, my wife has sent an urgent request—'

'I'm on my way back. I've spoken with Cynthia. She's left early and will meet us. Where's Lauren?'

Carlton glanced out the window. 'Right in front of me.'

'Let her know I'm five minutes out. Ten tops. You need to join us.'

'Terrance, I'm due . . .' Carlton stopped because Terrance had already cut the connection.

Carlton checked the kitchen clock. Four minutes. He rushed outside, called, 'Lauren, your father . . .'

The vice president's daughter swung around far enough to reveal a tear-streaked face. 'Go call your wife.'

Carlton breathed around the enormity of what the woman's words held. Then he rushed back inside. Climbed the stairs, entered the bedroom, crossed to the narrow side table he was using as a desk. He set his phone by the laptop and typed in the portal address. The password was his granddaughter's name followed by the string of letters and symbols contained in the text.

He watched the password dissolve and be replaced by a single blinking light. Counting down the seconds. There was no reason for his heart to be racing, or his hands to tremble as they did.

Carlton's family had never seemed more distant than when the dark web portal opened and they appeared. Neither his daughter Alexi nor his wife Marina shed tears. Yet their expression mirrored that of the vice president's daughter. Solemn and awestruck and nearly tragic in their shared intensity.

His wife said, 'You look good, sweetheart. Tired but good.'

Alexi agreed, 'Washington agrees with you, Daddy.'

Carlton demanded, 'What's wrong?'

'Nothing at all,' Marina replied.

'Truly?'

'Yes, my dearest.'

'Everything is fine, Daddy,' Alexi replied. 'Better than that.'

He felt his chest unlock. 'Where's my granddaughter?'

'Asleep.'

'She's OK?'

'She's fine, dear. Growing more beautiful with every passing day.'

Which was when the bedroom door opened, and Lauren entered. Without knocking. And stood there watching him. Solemn. Intent. He had not realized the young woman wore contact lenses until that moment. Lauren's tortoiseshell glasses enlarged her solemn gaze. Carlton thought the change was remarkable. Lauren lost the last vestiges of her wild-girl persona and fully became what she was now. A highly intelligent woman working hard to redefine herself.

Carlton basically spoke to everyone when he said, 'You've lost me.'

Marina said, 'Remember us talking about the barrier we've faced?'

'Of course.' It had been a topic of almost every conversation. 'Eleven months and counting.'

'It's gone.'

Carlton found himself unable to question his wife's announcement. Lauren's presence, the way she shared his wife's and daughter's solemn joy, fractured his thinking.

His wife continued, 'Dearest one, there's something you need to do.'

'For us,' Alexi said. 'For yourself. And for everyone else who's involved.'

'Call it a request from the heart,' Marina told him. 'Call it a demand. Whatever brings you to the point where you're willing to take this step.'

'It has to happen,' Lauren agreed. She walked over and set a tiny plastic envelope containing leaf dust on the table beside his laptop.

'Please, Daddy,' Alexi said. 'For all our sakes.'

Fifteen minutes later, the three of them took the same places they had occupied the previous evening. Cynthia's chair was empty, but only momentarily. Lauren assured her father that his wife was on final approach, and Terrance saw no need to question. Then they heard a car door slam and Terrance's wife rushed around the side of the house. 'Sorry, sorry. Traffic.'

Lauren reached for her mother's hand. 'All right?'

'Better than that,' Cynthia replied. 'But you know that already, don't you.'

'Oh, yes.' Lauren told her father, 'Daddy, it might be a good idea for Jadyn to be here too.'

The head of Terrance's security detail walked down the paving-stone path around the house and waited for Terrance to say, 'Join us.' When the agent was seated, Terrance launched straight in. 'My meeting with the president to let him know my next steps was canceled at the very last moment. The message was delivered by Agnes Pendalon.'

Cynthia said, 'I'm sorry, that name . . .'

Jadyn offered, 'Formerly the CIA's deputy chief of operations, now head of the investigative arm assigned to extinguish our group. She answers to General Skarren, head of defense intelligence, and Avri Rowe, the president's chief of staff. And through him, the president.'

Cynthia showed her husband a solemn, sorrowful gaze. 'That's it, then.'

'There's more,' Terrance said. 'According to Ms Pendalon, the president has instructed me to submit all speaking engagements to Avri for approval. My team is hereby ordered to refuse any and all requests for unscripted interviews. Everything I say, from this point forward, must be restricted to speeches written by Rowe's team.'

Carlton found himself able to pay careful attention to all the external elements in this conversation. Yet he mostly remained involved in registering precisely what was taking place on an internal level.

The extraordinary awareness. The continual expansion of contacts with other people.

The pressure.

The urgency.

Lauren said, 'That's insane.'

Cynthia said, 'They can't possibly expect you to agree.'

Terrance went on, 'I asked Ms Pendalon if the president wanted my resignation. She replied, "That depends."'

Carlton's only hard moment came then. Seated there, listening to the vice president disconnect from the role he had endured for four long years, Carlton sensed his wife and daughter reach out. Offering their support.

Terrance's next words were halted when Carlton huffed a half-cough, half-sob. 'Are you all right?'

Lauren replied, 'Carlton is fine, Daddy.'

Terrance inspected his daughter. 'Is he?'

'Fine and getting better.'

'You know this how?'

Reluctantly, gently, Carlton's wife and daughter drew away. Releasing him to focus upon the matters closer to hand. He said, 'I ingested the leaf.'

Terrance asked, 'When was this?'

'After you called. My wife and daughter contacted me. They said it was time.' Another hard breath. 'They were right.'

Terrance inspected the four of them in turn. Carlton, Cynthia, Lauren, Jadyn. He asked them all, 'Should I do this?'

Lauren's eyes widened with the same surprise Carlton felt. He watched the vice president's daughter open her mouth, ready herself to launch in, and . . .

Nothing. Not a peep.

Carlton nodded agreement to the daughter's silence. This was not telepathy in the traditional sense. Thought transference, verbal communication. Neither of these was the goal nor the gift. This was something far more profound. And powerful. All this was evident in the gentle insistence that halted Lauren's normal outburst.

His own realization arrived then. Strong as an electric shock. Yet gentle enough for him to accept it as a request. An unfinished concept. A glimpse into what might be the correct way forward. Not for him to merely accept and put in motion. Rather, asking him to fashion the concept into something workable.

Carlton was propelled out of his seat and across the patio. He stared at the forest's boundary and felt his political landscape undergo a seismic shift.

He had no idea how long he remained standing there. Time did not lose its significance. Not by any means. If anything, this realization or suggestion or whatever he wished to call it actually magnified the clock's importance.

When he was ready, Carlton walked back and seated himself. 'I apologize for the delay.'

Terrance nodded.

'The issue is not whether you should take this step. Sooner or later, I'm fairly certain you will decide the moment has arrived.'

Terrance asked, 'You're saying, I shouldn't ingest the leaf now?'

'No one can make that decision but you,' Cynthia replied. 'Certainly, if you want, do it.'

'We want this more than anything,' Lauren agreed.

Terrance asked Carlton, 'You have an alternative in mind?'

'It has to do with your next step,' Carlton replied.

'You mean, my candidacy.'

'There is a road we can take,' Carlton agreed. 'A compass heading that will define everything we do from this point forward.'

'*We* do,' Terrance repeated. 'You're with me?'

'I will do whatever you ask.'

'Will you run my campaign?'

'It would be my greatest honor,' Carlton replied.

'I want to set this course with full knowledge,' Terrance said. 'I need a clear perspective on shoals and storms ahead.'

'It's something I've always liked and admired about you,' Carlton said.

'So let's begin by you describing what you think this alternative course might look like,' Terrance said. 'In detail.'

Carlton felt the surge building with every word. He rode a wave of power so great it eliminated his ability to look beyond this gathering. He knew this might be their last opportunity to take time, proceed in careful stages, develop a shared vision. The wave of force was soon going to strike the political shoreline and begin breaking. Once that happened, they would all be racing for their lives.

In this one space, however, he found himself able to look *beyond* the coming campaign. What lay *beyond* this bend in time. A series of events that dwarfed even the plans to make Terrance Dale the next president of the United States.

Because that could very well happen. Carlton felt the resonance deep in his bones.

When he finished detailing their potential next steps, it was Terrance's turn to rise. Frown. Ponder. Get up from his chair. Pace.

Lauren reached out, took Carlton's hand, mouthed a silent *wow.*

Finally, Terrance resumed his seat and demanded, 'Everything you've laid out. This is for real?'

'All of it,' Carlton replied. 'The funds, advance team, PR structure, marketing group – they're all ready to go on your word.'

He paused, then, 'Have you told me everything?'

Lauren replied, 'Not even close.'

Terrance studied his daughter. 'Is it bad?'

'On the contrary,' Carlton replied.

Cynthia spoke then. 'Darling, you can trust him and us to tell you the truth at every turn. And the answer is, what you don't yet know is very, very good indeed.'

Terrance asked, 'What you're not telling me, does it come down to a deniability issue?'

'In a sense,' Carlton replied. 'It would be good if you can be as shocked and surprised as everyone else when it emerges. Which it will. Very soon.'

'Makes sense.'

'And one other thing,' Carlton said. 'They will be watching. Avri Rowe and his team will do their utmost to peel away any subterfuge and see if you are, well . . .'

'One of us,' Cynthia said.

'Joined,' Lauren offered. 'Part of what's about to happen.'

'Having nothing for them to find would help,' Carlton said. 'A great deal.'

Terrance smiled when Lauren reached out her free hand. 'Let's do this,' he said, 'Take the route you're suggesting. We can adjust course if or when required. A successful campaign is built on staying prepared to shift when the winds or currents . . .'

He stopped when his wife rose and slipped into his lap and embraced him.

Lauren said softly, 'Yay.'

'Speed is essential,' Carlton said. 'I've been pressured from all sides long before taking my own personal step. I spent all day laying out what we need for stage one. If you're in agreement, we need to gather the press so you can give your initial announcement before tomorrow's evening news.'

Jadyn checked his watch, then rose to his feet. 'Sir, excuse me, but you're due on the Senate floor in forty minutes.'

Terrance released his wife, rose to his feet, met Carlton's gaze, and said, 'Make it happen.'

FIFTEEN

When they reached the closest point to the crop circle, Val and Lynda and Sean lifted the chairs and carried them one by one to the central design. The only person who spoke was Theresa, the last of the three to arrive. She offered them a gentle, 'Thank you, dears. I really did want to be part of what is coming next.'

'Wouldn't be the same without you,' Sean replied.

The intense ticking clock was still present, but different. The stress and urgent push was replaced by a larger view, at least for Val. She felt as if they were entering a rushing tidal flow. A final breath, a pause to gather herself, before she was swept into the unknown.

Val stepped to one side and did her best to frame the scene in words. This close, the crop circle revealed a structure unlike anything she had ever seen. The grain was not simply mashed flat, pressed down to form the design. Instead, the strands were *woven*. Val turned in a slow circle, taking in the windless day, the china-blue sky, the people standing on the ridgeline's path above the White Horse, peering down at them. A concept came to her then, as if it had been shouted across some great distance, heard despite the hurricane forces.

Chrysalis.

In that instant, Val was flooded with a conviction that her months of sorrowful isolation held real purpose. Her situation was unique. The professional observer brought to the maximum level of intensity in this moment of moving on, rejoining, growing . . .

Wings.

When the signal came, it was sharp as a silent claxon.

She stood and saw the others had shifted to full alert. She had time for one clear thought, one final message to herself. *Remember.*

The transition carried none of the impact she had experienced in the stone circle. This time, the force held a gentle note. Intense, yet far from overwhelming.

It all came down to the dreams that until this very moment had never made sense.

Now she was back inside the beautiful realm. Only the absence of visual light held no significance. Sight as she knew it did not exist here. The intensity of experiencing life from an entirely new perspective opened her mind like a flower in bloom. A single word emerged from the midst of this gentle whirlwind, repeated over and over and over.

HELP.

Their next steps were crucial, she knew. Life or death. It all depended on their getting it right. Doing what was needed. Answering the plea. Before it was too late.

SIXTEEN

The very instant Kelly entered the therapist's inner office, she noticed the difference. For the first time in any of their sessions, Vivienne was not fully engaged.

Twice in the first five minutes, the therapist seemed to drift off. Not go to sleep, rather, she just . . . went away.

Finally, Kelly asked, 'Is everything all right?'

'Obviously not.' She rose to her feet and started for the corner kitchenette. 'Coffee?'

'Sure. Black.'

'I feel like I'm being pulled in two different directions today.' She slipped a coffee-pod into the machine, checked the water level, placed a cup under the nozzle, and hit the button. 'No matter how difficult the session, I am normally able to step away and enter the next meeting like I am moving to another room. Today I am unable to fully focus. This happens so rarely I can't even recall the last time. I apologize.'

'No problem.' Kelly accepted the cup. 'Do you want to cancel?'

'Absolutely not.' Vivienne settled back into her chair. 'All right. The time for distractions is over. Let's get back to where we left off last session.'

'Paranoid personality disorder,' Kelly said. 'PPD.'

'Are there any thoughts you'd like to share?'

'Yes. Why now? Is there some wrong move I've made—'

'Please don't use that word, wrong.' Sharp now. With her. 'In my opinion, you and Stanley are handling the impossible. And doing so while both of you remain involved in active duty.'

'I'm not stepping back from my duties.'

'And I am not suggesting you do so.' When she lifted her cup from the side table, Vivienne's hand visibly shook. 'There is no road map for how to help you deal with this trauma. Your experience is totally new. Our job is to see you through this healing process. Once we're on the other side, the three of us should take time to examine the process. Do a full sit-rep. In case there is another such instance.'

Kelly nodded. 'I see that. But my question stays the same. Why PPD, and why now?'

'I am seeking to apply elements that are designed around other cases. You should view this as part of the healing process. I make suggestions. You must decide whether or not my analysis fits. I told you during our first session that we are walking this road together. Stanley too, of course. But you are the individual in a leadership role. Your responsibilities include the analyzing of incoming data and reaching a valid conclusion . . .'

Kelly saw it happen again. The therapist was abruptly pulled away. Kelly felt something akin to jealousy, having someone else's session invade their private space. She probed with the same words. 'But why now?'

Vivienne shuddered, focused, and still needed a moment to find her way back. 'You and Stanley have been using the same word to describe the current situation faced by the newcomers to your team. The ones who should in principle still be connected. And yet they too have become shut out. Except for this one element.'

Kelly nodded again. 'Pressure.'

'By this, you clearly mean there is a sense of an impending crisis. A juncture where action will be required. Correct?'

'OK, yes, but I still—'

'When that happens, when the crisis is revealed, *you are alone*. The friendship and alliance you feel with Stanley will not enter the crisis situation with you. You will be forced apart. That is what it means to be a leader. The solitary individual. Pointing the way ahead.'

Kelly felt the all-too-familiar sense of being struck from an unexpected direction. So hard, so sudden, she wished she could draw back. Erase everything she had been saying. Take back her questions. Let Vivienne drift away into whatever traumatic fog she had carried into this session.

Instead, the therapist continued, 'At the crisis point, Stanley becomes one of your team. Yes, of course, a senior member. A lieutenant, if you will. But he is there to follow your lead. Just like all the others who make up your frontline force.'

Kelly could not have spoken even if she wanted. Air had somehow vacated the room.

'Your responsibility is to track the right course. Your team relies on this. Which means you must be able to see the full picture. Without any bias that is defined by the stress and hardship and psychic wounds you have endured.' Vivienne leaned forward. 'This is a multi-dimensional issue. Many perspectives, many questions, many possible courses of action. If you are willing to look beyond what you personally feel is right.'

Kelly managed, 'In this case, we *are* right.'

'And that is not the point. What if your perspective and your plans are all founded upon where this other group were months ago? What happens if they have moved on, progressed to a different situation, one that you are unable to see because . . .'

Vivienne straightened.

Kelly started to ask what was wrong. Then she heard the faint drumbeat of footsteps. The outer door opened and slammed shut. A man shouted Kelly's name. Someone pounded on the office door. Another shout, this one loud enough for Kelly to recognize Rabbit's voice.

Vivienne touched the button on her table that triggered the electronic lock.

Rabbit rushed in. 'You've got to come now.' Kelly's rise from the seat was too slow for him. He reached out, made a fist in the space between them, said to Vivienne, 'We've been calling for almost an hour. You need an emergency alert on your phone service.'

Kelly was almost grateful for the reason to escape. She followed him through the empty outer office and rushed to keep up. Down the main stairwell, through the lobby, out to where a black Tahoe waited. Lights imbedded in the front grill flashed an alert. They started moving before Kelly had her door shut.

Rabbit started straight in, describing the moment when every single one of his new team members came back online. That was how he described it. As though they had all been suffering from a momentary lapse in connection.

She did her best to both listen and prepare. But Kelly was still recovering from the session. She knew without a doubt that the fuse was burning; the transition Rabbit and his team had been anticipating was upon them. Given everything else they faced – Terrance Dale coming out against them, the mission team trapped in a Canadian military prison – the timing could not be worse.

Just the same, Kelly had the definite sense that she was missing something vital. But when her vision fully cleared and she could parse the events and focus on the unseen, it was too late. By that point, all the world had changed.

SEVENTEEN

Ten minutes after the vice president departed, Carlton had only made it as far as the pool's perimeter. He paced and thought and planned. Four times his phone buzzed with incoming messages. But he left it in his pocket. The required next steps had to be precisely timed. The right people informed, the signals and the alerts all made in precise tandem with the upcoming announcement . . .

He sensed a sudden shift in unseen winds. Then he became intensely connected to Val. Not seeing it through her eyes or anything like that. Something totally different. He remained there in Washington, staring across the pool's glistening waters. And yet he was also in England, the experience so vivid he saw the gigantic white horse carved into the hillside, smelled the grain woven into some incredible design beneath their feet, and then . . .

A message arrived. From where, he sensed an enormous distance, an inability to completely shape their position, or even who or what they were . . . All Carlton could say for certain was how the message came through loud and clear.

HELP.

When he was able to refocus, Carlton was mildly astonished that the experience had not flattened him on the grassy rear lawn. Just left him prostrate, helpless as a newborn, blinking dully at passing clouds. Thankfully, though, he had managed to settle in a poolside chair before being completely and utterly overwhelmed.

Call it what it was. He had been assaulted.

He had no idea if others felt as he did. When he regained control of thoughts and limbs, he lost that sense of bonding. It faded in the same tempo as his returning strength. That momentary sense of intimate connection was so intense, so beautiful, he could have wept at its departure.

Early in his career, Carlton had attended a movers-and-shakers conference in Sedona. Toward the end of his stay, he had participated in a pre-dawn hike into the high desert. They stopped on a ridgeline for coffee and power bars just as the rising sun extinguished the silver wash of stars.

One moment, all was gentle pastels and birdsong. The next, the sun rose over eastern peaks and transformed everything. Carlton had felt the shocking transition in his bones. The sudden wash of heat and light had blistered his senses.

What he had just experienced carried the same intensity. That and more.

Cynthia came out then, followed closely by Lauren. 'Are you all right?'

Carlton managed to lift one arm off the chair and see-saw his hand. So-so.

'I think tea with a good dollop of honey is in order. Yes? Good. It was already brewing when we were impacted. Lauren, could you . . .'

'On it.'

'Thank you, dear.' Cynthia pulled over a chair and seated herself. 'I can't imagine what that must have been like, coming so soon after you joined.'

He managed, 'Blinding.'

'I'm sure it was.'

'What *happened*?'

'This is a first for me as well. I suspect for everyone. So my reply is mostly guesswork . . . Oh, thank you, dear.'

Lauren handed Denton a mug, then stood and made sure he could hold it steady. Which he did only by using both hands. The rough ceramic helped anchor him. As did the first sip. Ginger tea with honey. A new favorite. The elixir was hot and sweet and helped enormously. 'Thank you.'

Cynthia waited until Lauren pulled over another chair and joined them. Then, 'My impression was, everything we've experienced over these long, silent months has been readying us for this moment.'

'Now I know what a butterfly feels like, flying for the very first time,' Lauren agreed.

Carlton asked Lauren, 'When I saw you out there on the lawn. Before your father arrived. Was this the same?'

'Not at all,' she replied. 'But connected. Like that prepared me for this.'

'The same power,' Cynthia said. 'But this was a far more forceful joining.'

'A forceful joining,' Lauren repeated. 'Mom, you're a poet in the making.'

Cynthia said, 'You see your next steps, don't you?'

'Yes. I do.' Carlton handed Lauren the mug, thanked her, and levered himself to his feet. 'I had better get to work.'

EIGHTEEN

'There was a distinct before and after,' Rabbit said. 'Before, the link was total. Like the past eleven months never existed. And a lot more besides.'

'Explain this new status,' Agnes said. 'I want the full download.'

Kelly spoke for the first time since Rabbit had started his debriefing. 'Ma'am, excuse me, but I advise you to wait on this.'

'Stanley has already briefed you?'

'No, and for the same reason I'm suggesting he not do this now.'

Agnes barked, 'Explain.'

'We know our new team members have rejoined fully. We know the opposition is out there planning something. We need to determine next steps. Having Stanley detail what he and his group touched on and then lost . . .' She was halted by Rabbit shaking his head. 'Something wrong?'

'We didn't lose it entirely,' Rabbit said. 'We just lost the ability to bond and observe with that other group.'

Agnes said, 'Define what you mean by that term, you *lost.*'

'Ma'am, Kelly is right. We're not certain, and even if we were, we couldn't put it in words. Not yet.'

Agnes reluctantly assented. 'All right. Give me what you can.'

Kelly thought Rabbit did a pro's job of describing the moment his new team members reconnected. He sat to Kelly's right, facing the screen that dominated the side wall. All of his new team and some of the original crew – those blinded the same instant as Kelly and Rabbit – were gathered around a conference table behind him, nineteen in all. They faced the camera, and the screen now split to show five others. Agnes and Skarren and Grey Mathers and Avri Rowe were joined by Darren Cotton, the head of Kelly's physical and online intel group. Her other second in command, Barry Riggs, was still held in Canada's version of military detention.

Just the same, Kelly had difficulty focusing on what Rabbit was saying. Despite the fact the gathered brass would soon demand her assessment. Want her input regarding next steps.

Kelly's attention kept switching back to Avri Rowe. For the first time ever, the president's chief of staff was not fully engaged. Normally, Avri's concentration was total. He had the ability to maintain a sniper's focus. Today, his attention was continually being drawn to events outside her field of vision.

What was more, Kelly was fairly certain Skarren knew the reason. The head of defense intelligence bore a frown that aged him. He showed them the troubled gaze of a general whose battlefield plans were in tatters. Nothing they had revealed in this briefing suggested a threat of that magnitude.

Yet.

When Rabbit went silent, Agnes said what Kelly was expecting. And dreading. 'OK, Kelly, give us your take.'

'There are two definite issues here. First, the barrier keeping most or all telepaths from full connectivity is gone, at least for this moment. And two, they have a new ability. Everything else is conjecture.'

'They can shut us out now,' Skarren said.

Kelly nodded. 'Our greatest potential source of intel is lost. The question is do they no longer need to communicate via phones and computers, or have they also gained an ability to telepath in words?'

The general asked, 'Stanley, what's your take?'

'We're back to what Kelly said earlier, sir. We just don't know.' Rabbit gestured to the others in his group. 'Our links are stronger, but verbal communication is still beyond our scope. For now, anyway.'

Kelly continued, 'We're making solid inroads on unsealing their sat phones and dark web comm links. Our biggest hope is that any such transition to verbal communication will be gradual. If so, we can hopefully track their progress by way of existing comm links.'

Darren added, 'The crop circle group has apparently split up. The jet that brought Val Garnier and her associate from the US has left Bristol on its return flight.'

Skarren asked, 'Should we target a strike?'

Agnes said, 'Our primary strike team is still being held by the Canadian military. There is the risk the Canadians allied to this group are looking for just such a provocation. Something they can use as a justification to create a public outcry. On a global scale.'

Darren said, 'Since their flight took off, they've been in regular contact with their allies in New York.'

'Calling on lines we can track,' Agnes said. 'They're operating out in the open now. Which can only mean one thing. Anything we do at this stage will result in them going public.'

'So what you're telling me is there's a secret group equipped with potentially strengthened or new abilities that are sitting pretty in England, while another group is heading into our heartland,' Skarren said. 'We have no idea what they're planning, and we can't risk bringing them in for questioning. Could this possibly get any worse?'

'I'm afraid so.' Avri Rowe accepted a sheet of paper from someone off-screen, read it swiftly, then announced, 'Vice President Terrance Dale has scheduled a national news conference for tomorrow afternoon. This is a direct contradiction to my instructions that he not speak to anyone without prior approval.'

Skarren groaned. 'He's going to announce his candidacy.'

'The situation here inside the White House is one step removed from full-on panic,' Rowe said. 'Agnes, Skarren, you may need to handle things. I'll join you when and if I can.'

His screen went blank.

NINETEEN

As soon as their vision cleared, Val, Denton, and Lynda left the crop circle for Bristol Airport. It was just the three of them now, rushing to luxuriate their way across the Atlantic. Greg and his gang were not moving. They were planted in the Pusey Vale for the duration. Taking over a pair of homes they found advertised on Airbnb. There to hold vigil on the crop circle. Twenty-four seven.

They arrived to find the Gulfstream's door open and engines revving. Val spent the first few hours of their flight writing her version of the Avebury events. She only got as far as describing the town of standing stones and the initial events that reshaped their world. Literally.

When she paused for a meal, Lynda insisted she stop. Rest. Prepare for what waited for them upon landing. Val only protested mildly, and mostly from habit.

They landed at Cedar Falls, Iowa, at one eighteen in the afternoon. The view on descent was of flat country turned golden in the early autumn, with rivers cutting shimmering ribbons through corn country. Val thought she could actually hear the ticking clock. Which was nuts, since the jet's digital timers made no sound. Just the same, the drumbeat of pressure propelled them all.

Following a text message from Denton, they rented a Buick Enclave from the airport Hertz and drove to the local Red Roof motel. Val showered off the trip, dressed in relatively clean clothes, and was outside when the others emerged. Greeting Denton was hurried and mostly silent, as all of them were captured by the rising sense of urgency. They set off north on the 218, speeding past Waverly, heading toward Charles City. Val actually found herself enjoying the shared intensity. Their task was simple enough. It required no great skillset to serve on this particular front line. Other than, of course, the ability to drive into corn country and sign contracts and spend money. A lot of money.

Their destination was a new agricultural compound on the outskirts of Osage. The construction site was so large they spotted the dust cloud three miles out. At its heart were six grain silos that glinted tall and imposing. They were bunched in tightly together, big as office buildings, topped by steel scaffolding and pipes twenty feet in diameter.

As Lynda pulled through the hurricane fencing and stopped by the guard station, Denton told her, 'Remember what they always say. Size doesn't matter.'

Lynda rolled down her window, gave the name of their contact, then said, 'It matters. It matters a lot.'

They were directed to a parking lot holding several hundred vehicles, most of them dusty pickups. The three men headed their way were all of a kind – big and solid and self-assured. They wore jeans and boots and hard hats and matching grins. The elder man said, 'We're looking for Dennis Hayes.'

'It's Denton,' he said. 'Mr Juniper?'

'Bob to anybody willing to come all this way.' He shook their hands, introduced his pals, said, 'We got a call yesterday from a nice-sounding lawyer lady.'

'That would be Connor Breach.'

'I have to tell you, that conversation was one for the books.' The trio shared another grin. 'We figured she got her wires crossed. On account of how she claims you want to buy our new silos.'

'That is correct,' Denton said. 'We do.'

'Well, all I got to say is, you've made a wasted trip. Because they're not for sale.' He swept a hand behind him, taking in the four warehouses, six silos, and three more factory-size buildings still under construction. 'All of this is a turn-key project.'

The smallest of the three added, 'We're not about to let one of our competitors waltz in and set up shop in our compound.'

Denton asked their spokesman, 'You're the site manager?'

'That's right. And this man to my left here is Rus Atkins, project engineer. His company, Unified Construction, is the world's top silo builder. He'll see you right. Go ahead, Rus. Tell these fine folks what you can do for them.'

He was a dark-haired man, bulky as an aging linesman, whose

sweaty face was streaked with grime. 'What you see there are bolted steel silos. Each holds a capacity of two thousand tons. High precision, good adaptability, easy assembly. The underlay is solid steel scaffolding set on nine feet of poured reinforced concrete.' He pointed to the metal webbing far overhead. 'All six are serviced by high-speed top feeds, same for the discharges. Super-strong conveyor systems link them to the warehouses. Their interiors are fully ventilated, temperature controlled, the works.'

'Rus is as good as his word,' Juniper said. 'If he claims he can get your rigs up and running in six months, he'll do it.'

'Eight tops,' the engineer said.

'We don't have eight months,' Denton replied. 'We need them now.'

'Sir, I don't know how much clearer I can make it—'

'How much would a turn-key operation cost? I'm talking about just the silos and their underpinning. Not your warehouses.'

Juniper frowned at Rus, who replied, 'Ball park is all I could possibly give you without a full assessment of your land.'

'Ball park is fine.'

'Six silos of this size?'

'All six.'

'With foundations and top overlays, you're looking at a final cost of between fifty and fifty-five million.'

Denton said, 'I offer you one hundred and fifty million dollars.'

The trio lost their grins.

'Cash,' Denton said. 'I assumed our attorney confirmed our ability to pay.'

'Sir, Mr . . . We'll need to check with our board.'

'They won't like you encroaching on our project, no matter how much you pay,' the third man said. 'Not one bit.'

Juniper was less confident. 'A hundred-million-dollar profit is a very persuasive argument.'

Denton replied, 'We don't want use of your land.'

'What, you're going to *move* them?'

'We are. Yes.'

Juniper laughed. Sort of. A single bark of angry protest. 'How many choppers do you aim on bringing here?'

'That's my concern,' Denton said.

Rus demanded, 'Do you have the *slightest* idea how much one of those silos weigh?'

'Same answer.' Denton held up his hand, silencing them. 'Gentlemen, the contract will be with you shortly. The transfer of funds will take place as soon as you supply your bank details. At the top of the contract's first page, you'll find a clause stating that if the silos are still on your property twenty-four hours after signing, they return to your possession. And you keep the money.'

Val thought the trio's ability to share expressions, from grinning mirth to open-mouth astonishment, was hilarious. She dared not glance at Lynda for fear her own grin might break out.

Denton asked, 'Do we have a deal?'

TWENTY

Carlton had almost forgotten how much fun it was to be this busy. His day started well before dawn. Despite the hour, he entered the kitchen to find freshly brewed coffee in the thermos, another pot ready to brew, and breakfast items on the counter. Cynthia was already working at the dining-room table, which had apparently become her secondary office. She had a desk in the library, but that had been taken over by Lauren, who was pushing hard on her thesis, trying to complete the first draft before, as she put it, they entered Outer Earth Orbit. Which, given the state of affairs they all faced, Carlton thought was genuinely funny.

There were two reasons why Carlton was moving forward without doubt or hesitation. Communicating with some realm that redefined human existence, and accepting it calmly, all came down to these two factors.

The first was that they remained united in a way that challenged many of the assumptions which had previously defined Carlton's life. He was his own man. And yet the flow of new events was also binding him to a purpose far greater than his work, or even his life. And the new reality thrilled him.

The second was that they all were part of this. The momentum, the challenge, the great pressing need. And every now and then, something linked him to the others in a new way. As if these almost daily moments were part of whatever it meant to be redefined.

Just like now.

Midmorning found him in the kitchen refreshing his mug and debating whether he should make a second breakfast. He had eaten a yogurt and fruit concoction at half past five. It was almost ten and his stomach was growling. The prospect of another two hours until lunch was unappealing in the extreme.

When it happened.

Carlton experienced a gentle yet insistent alert. Like the faint chiming of crystal bells. Or a beautiful melody being sung in a distant room.

His sat phone rang.

He carried two phones with him everywhere. The sat phone was still the method of choice for team communications. His new iPhone was for the rising tide of political work. Though it was increasingly difficult to tell where one segment of his life ended and the other began.

'This is Carlton.'

'Hi, Carlton. This is Sean Stiles.' The man's unfamiliar voice carried a hint of laughter. 'By any chance, have you heard of me?'

'Denton has mentioned you. Several times, in fact.' As in, Dr Sean Stiles was the former husband of Ryan, the woman who had almost wrecked Denton's life. Twice. And then he had co-piloted the plane he and Denton were on before an Air Force jet blew it out of the sky. 'Are you still in Canada?'

'I was until recently.' Sean sounded like someone who preferred meeting almost everything with a smile. 'I wound up playing the sort-of mayor. Manager. Janitor-in-chief. Do you mind if we leave the rest of our catch-up for later? I don't know about you, but we all feel like we're racing the clock.'

'On that we can certainly agree. Who is we?'

'I'm part of the team now stationed at the crop circle. We want you to call the press, alert them to the next seismic event.'

'Here in DC?'

'No. Cedar Falls.'

'Where?'

'Eastern Iowa.' Sean finally released his laugh. 'I know that's not the first place you'd expect as the center of a world-shaking event. But we don't have any choice in the matter.'

Carlton reached for pad and pen. 'Tell me what you need.'

TWENTY-ONE

Through the long afternoon hours, Val and Denton took turns checking in with the geek team. Val's term. They were based in Bali of all places, where they had acquired a large compound in the island's central hills. Surrounded by tea plantations and tribal people who were born and raised to ask no questions about rich visitors. Val liked how the brief conversations via their sat phone remained in total harmony with the unspoken links that continued to build.

The sun was setting on corn country when the bank's regional director drove up, shook hands with the trio who continued to cluster a dozen paces or so removed from the three crazy people. The bank VP waved a sheaf of papers in the air as he talked. Then all four walked over and confirmed the sale had gone through.

They made the day's final call to Bali over the car's speakers while driving back into town. Denton confirmed, 'We're all set for ten tomorrow morning. Your team better be on time. Else we're going to be out a hundred and fifty mil.'

'Not to mention being the butt of Iowa jokes for a generation,' Lynda added.

The guy on the other end was named Chakkan, a Thai who had been studying electrical engineering at MIT until he was swept up in the global transformation. 'Who's that talking?'

'A lady with her head screwed on right,' Lynda replied.

'Glad somebody's is. When we're done here, maybe you should move to Bali, teach my geeks how to walk in step.'

'The location is tempting,' Lynda said. 'As for a long-term assignment supervising techies, I'd rather herd goats in Baghdad.'

Val had met Chakkan prior to her first and only trip on what was now referred to as the plywood rocket, which she counted as one of her top-ten lifetime experiences. She would have paid good money for a second trip. But soon as they landed, the rocket and a warehouse full of support gear had been blown up, on account of how Agnes Pendalon and her assault team were on close approach.

Chakkan said, 'When you two come visit us here in paradise, be sure and bring the lady. We could use some clear thinking for a change.'

'The name's Lynda,' she said. 'I've always wanted to see Bali.'

'Talk to Val. We've been trying to get her over since forever.'

'Soon as this is over,' Val said.

'Speaking of which, I sure hope you're sticking around for the Iowa fireworks before you head out for the LA segment of this crazy mission.'

The three of them exchanged a look. Val asked, 'What segment would that be?'

Chakkan went quiet, then, 'Uh-oh.'

Val demanded, 'What is it?'

'Forget I said anything. I don't want to get on the wrong side of our folks squatting in the crop circle.'

Denton's tone hardened. 'Chakkan.'

He went sulky. 'What.'

'Talk.'

When he remained silent, Val pressed, 'I thought the silo's contents were being handled by Richie and his pals.'

More silence.

Denton did not use volume to command, 'Tell us and tell us now.'

Val and Lynda gathered in Denton's room and watched Terrance Dale announce his candidacy for president. They then went across the street and down one block to a roadside grill. The steaks were beyond good. The place was packed; Val assumed most of the patrons worked at the construction site. Big men and women, full of swagger and loud laughter, mostly out for a good time. She and her pals were the focus of attention while they ate. Theirs was the only silent table. Denton and Lynda were still coming to terms with all that Chakkan had shared regarding their next assignment. But something else kept Val quiet.

As she finished her meal, Val felt it all come together on an internal level. The intensity grew to where the shouted conversations, the jukebox, the laughter, even her friends drew far away. It was just her, sitting there, waiting. If she could have managed to speak at that moment, she would have told the others, *Incoming*.

Denton's sat phone rested on the table between his plate and the window. It buzzed just as the waitress replenished their coffee. He checked the readout, said, 'It's our pals at the crop circle. I better take this outside.'

'I'll pay the bill,' Lynda offered. She waited until Denton stepped away to ask Val, 'You OK there?'

But everything was converging to the point where Val could no longer respond.

She was only mildly aware that Lynda remained standing by the table for a time, watching her worriedly before heading to the bar. Val's attention was gently but forcibly turned away. Not so much inwardly as toward a new joining.

And everything about this experience was definitely new. She still sat in the restaurant. She could feel the hard varnished chair. Her left hand remained settled upon the scarred wooden table. A streetlight cast a yellow glow over the empty seats across from her. But what Val really saw was the crop circle.

She was joined now to the three people on duty. Greg was there, along with Sean and Theresa. The three were all mildly surprised at her arrival, and yet showed her a clear sense of being welcomed. Which was exactly how Val felt. Astonished and comfortable in equal measure.

Sean was talking with Denton on the sat phone, giving precise instructions for the step that was about to take place. Addresses, purchase details, coordinating with Connor who was also on the line. Sean cut the phone connection and spoke aloud to Val. 'Greg and the others just received one of those unequivocal alerts. You need to go with them. On this trip to never-never land.'

'I understand.' And she did. The words were scarcely a whisper, her lips barely moving. But speaking verbally separated the words from her mental jumble and sent them out in precise form. 'It scares me.'

'Of course it does.' There was a signature alert, like the mental version of a phone chime. Sean lifted his face, as if sniffing the wind, then asked, 'Chakkan, you there?'

'You bet. Hi, Val. I'm scared too.'

'Looks like there will be eight of you.'

Greg stepped in close. 'It's nine and you know it.'

Sean showed a rare level of concern. 'Your going will break your mother's heart.'

'Not if she ingests the leaf,' Greg replied. 'Which she should have done. Months ago.'

Sean did not disagree. 'It's not the leaf. It's releasing her hold on the past.'

'Mom has never had control,' Greg countered. 'Which is what stresses her out. Wanting what she can't have. It's time, though. And Mom feels it. She just needs to understand there is a whole globe of people willing to help.'

'If she wants to talk with another woman who's been where she is, sort of, have her call.' Val had never met the woman, but knew the stories. How Greg's mother had shaped her world around caring for the physically disabled son. How she now felt cast adrift by the transition her son and husband had both undergone. Val felt herself gently being pulled away. 'I have to go.'

'Me too,' Chakkan agreed. 'Hey, thanks. It's been wild.'

'Move fast, be ready,' Greg shouted across the growing distance. 'We leave in four days.'

Val emerged from her semi-trance just as a handsome lug in jeans and cowboy boots approached her table. 'Come on, darling. The jukebox is playing our song.'

She found it remarkably difficult to frame the words. Like her mouth was recovering from a dose of Novocain. 'Sorry. Don't dance.'

He wore an oversized rodeo buckle and a white shirt with oyster-shell buttons. He was handsome enough in a rawboned fashion. Tall and dark-haired and very self-assured. 'Lady as fine-looking as you? Now I know that ain't true.'

Val shaped each word with immense care. 'What I meant to say was I'm not dancing with you.'

'Well, at least let me buy you a drink.' He hiked a leg over the back of Denton's empty chair and dropped down. 'Least I can do.'

She was finally able to focus on him, which meant a vestige of her previous extended awareness swept in his direction. She did not just see the hidden edge beneath his good-old-boy charm. She was also very aware of the force binding him to six men gathered by the bar, the way they readied themselves to shift forward in unison, their pack-like hunger for the fight to come. It was all clear as the dawn sky she had just left behind. 'I'm good, thanks.'

Lynda started back from the bar just as Denton returned from his call. Val's two friends were clearly alarmed by the man's presence. He pretended not to notice. 'You're better than that. And I always did like a challenge.'

Val lifted one hand, halting Denton and Lynda's approach and silencing their concerns. She said, 'It's Carl, isn't it? Married to Stacey? No, sorry. Stacey's your daughter. Nine years old next week.'

He lost his grin. 'How'd you know—'

'And you're going to miss her birthday. Again. But Connie's used to holding up your end when you're on a job. Isn't that so?'

He was grim now. Intent. 'Who've you been talking to?'

'You were in a fight five months ago. Started just like the one you and your pals are planning on here. You wound up in jail overnight, got off with a warning. But you also received a caution when you showed up for work the next day.' Her ability to read the man's script was fading fast. Val found it easier to talk now. A little. 'One more sign of trouble and you're off the job.'

Thankfully, when Val went quiet, Lynda offered, 'Think on what it means, the three of us knowing what we do.'

'Them rumors we heard back on site. The crazy talk about you and your pals.' He rose to his feet, fists bunched, red-faced. Trapped. 'Another bunch of feds sent down to mess with our heads.'

Denton said, 'We're not the ones causing trouble, though, are we?'

'Let us buy you and your pals a drink,' Lynda offered.

'I don't want nothing from the feds except to be left alone,' the guy snarled.

'Sounds like a plan,' Denton said. 'We're leaving now.'

Val rose to her feet. 'Be sure and tell Connie I said hello.'

TWENTY-TWO

Kelly watched Terrance Dale announce his intention to run for president with all of her team. Their new ops center occupied an entire building in the Pentagon City office park. Thirty-three well-equipped private apartments filled the top five floors, enough for everyone who wished to reside there. Fully equipped gym. Rooftop pool. And a theater-sized conference room where they now gathered. Rabbit's group were clustered over to her right. The bottom left section, three rows from the front, was empty. Waiting for the team still trapped inside a Canadian military prison.

She had known Terrance was going to announce. The afternoon had contained a series of alerts, or warnings, or proclamations of doom. Whatever. But this was different. Seated on the front row with Agnes and Grey Mathers and Darren. Listening and watching as this man, this supposed ally to their president, threatened to shift the Earth's axis. Midway through the pundit's analysis, Kelly left the arena. She did not enter her apartment planning to sleep. It was simply time for a strategic retreat.

The next morning, Kelly brought the day's grim finality with her into the therapist's outer office. She did not sit down. No chair could hold her just then. She paced, not moving so much as expelling energy. Captured by forces beyond her control. On the one hand, she dreaded the coming session. On the other, she needed to let go. Release. Begin the sorting process. Dig for clarity. It was either that or explode.

Rabbit emerged. Nodded once. Started to speak. Then he headed for the door.

Kelly asked, 'You OK?'

He opened the door, hesitated, then said, 'I needed this. And I hated it more.'

It was as close to a confession as either had come. 'You took the words straight from my mouth.'

A single nod and he was gone.

When she entered the inner sanctum, the therapist greeted her with, 'Kelly, good. Come sit down.'

'I need to stand.'

'Very well.' If Vivienne was disturbed by Kelly's position, she gave no sign. 'Back to the topic of our last session.'

'Today I need to focus on sorting through everything that's happening.'

'I intend to. But first we need to establish a foundation for moving forward. And that means completing the previous discussion.'

Kelly began pacing. 'You said you weren't certain PPD was a condition that actually applied to me.'

'That is correct. But you can't have a clear view or make a clear decision about this without my final point.'

Kelly found it interesting how the room's larger space did not increase the distance she covered. If anything, her pacing became tighter. Three steps, swing about, back again. 'Go ahead, then.'

'The majority of our discussions have started from the moment you lost your ability to connect.' Vivienne held to her usual strength and calm, at complete odds with Kelly's tight pacing. 'For us to form this foundation you want for examining the current situation, we first need to look further back.'

Kelly slowed.

'I am not speaking about the death of your fiancé. Not directly. What I want you to consider is your initial contact with your superior. Agnes Pendalon.'

Kelly halted. Remained in mid-stride. Staring at the side wall.

'At the moment of greatest loss and agony, this woman offered you a focus. A direction for your rage. A target. An enemy. She revealed that your man was murdered by a drug lord who had fashioned telepaths to suit his aims. You returned from that mission and in your moment of bitter vindication, Agnes Pendalon expanded your viewpoint. She invited you to see all telepaths through that very same lens. All of them became your next enemy. Why? Because she said so.'

Kelly was not ready for this. Having the therapist strip away the room's air. Freeze her lungs. Halt Kelly's ability to even blink.

'Ever since that moment, your life has been spent taking aim. You claim this is your own design. And perhaps it is. But for us to arrive at a point of true healing, it is time for you to question this.' Vivienne's voice carried the same soft drone. Almost silken in quality. 'You need to acknowledge the role she has played in refashioning your life. You need to *question* this. You need to step back and determine your own next steps—'

'I have to go.' Kelly wheeled about and started for the door.

Vivienne merely touched the control unlocking the door and said, 'Until next time.'

Kelly rushed through the outer office, pushed through the stairwell door, took three steps, halted. Leaned against the cold concrete wall. Gasped for the breath she could not find inside the therapist's office. She had no idea what might have happened if Vivienne had tried to keep her caged. Her duty weapon was in her purse. There was no telling where she might have taken aim.

TWENTY-THREE

Val and the others returned to Denton's room and watched a CNN rerun of the vice president's news conference in Denton's motel room. Afterwards Denton shifted between stations, checking out the talking heads, all of whom said little more than how shocked they were, and how Terrance Dale did not stand a chance. Denton and Lynda kept glancing Val's way, not asking if she was all right or what happened back in the roadhouse.

Val was grateful for their silence. She needed to tell them, but not yet. There was too much to sort through, bring into some form of mental order. Finally, she bid them a good night, returned to her room, and dreamed of beings who could not fathom the concept of sight.

The three of them watched the news conference a second time over breakfast at a local diner. When they returned to the car, Denton offered to drive. Wordlessly, Lynda tossed him the keys and settled into the passenger seat. He and Lynda spent the journey marveling over how their work and the vice president's announcement all came together. Absorbing the reality of fitting themselves into something so monumental a new presidential candidacy was just another part of the day's puzzle.

Val remained silent.

They arrived at the site with fifty-two minutes to spare. This morning, the parking lot held twice as many vehicles as the previous day. A crowd of several hundred people clustered between the lot and the construction site's fencing.

'I guess this is what passes for entertainment in corn country,' Denton said.

Lynda replied, 'If I heard somebody was planning to lift a thousand-ton silo—'

'Six silos,' Val corrected. 'Two thousand tons.'

'Right. That or lose a hundred and fifty million dollars now sitting in an escrow account, you bet your bippy I'd be out here too.'

The three senior construction site managers and the bank VP stood by the open main gate. With them were five newcomers, three men and two women, all wearing sunglasses and nice executive-style clothes and pinched expressions.

Denton reached for his door. 'We should probably go over and greet the suits.'

'No, wait,' Val said. 'There's something I need to tell you.'

Denton checked his watch. 'Chakkan and his team are about to make history—'

Lynda broke in with, 'Does this have to do with last night?'

'It does. Yes.'

'Shut your door, Denton. The suits can wait. Go ahead, Val.'

Val thought she did a poor job describing her experience while seated inside the roadhouse. When she finished, she wondered if this was going to remain an ongoing problem. Trying to fit these occurrences into words never meant to cover such events.

Lynda leaned against the side door, shifting her gaze back and forth between Denton and Val. Denton observed Val in the rearview mirror and tapped two fingers on the steering wheel, as if keeping time with Val's words. He held that position until she went quiet. Then he turned fully around, settling one leg on the hand brake, facing her. He said, 'What I'm hearing is, Sean and Greg asked if you'd come along for the ride, and you said yes.'

She nodded. Leave it to the forensic accountant to cut right to the core. 'They didn't *ask* anything. There was no *request.* Learning about the team's composition formed just one part of a much larger . . . I don't know what to call it.'

'Event works for me,' Lynda said quietly.

'There are probably a dozen people who would be better serving on point,' Val went on. 'A thousand. But this sense of resonance was so powerful, the whole issue of doubt or fear or whatever you want to call it, none of that had any place.'

As Denton and Lynda absorbed what she had just told them, the group they were ignoring became increasingly irate. Val watched as the bank manager started waving his sheaf of papers, just like the previous afternoon. Fourteen hours and several eons ago.

Denton said, ‘Promise me you’ll come back in one piece, Val. You’re too precious a friend to lose. Just because you get some message that pulls everything together doesn’t mean you can go out and get yourself dead. Promise me that.’

Val thought Denton had the gentlest smile she’d ever seen on a man. ‘Promise.’ Hoping it was so. Truly frightened. Despite everything she had just said. Terrified.

Denton asked, ‘You sure you’re up for this gig?’

She liked the man’s timeless manner enough to say, ‘Connor is a very lucky lady.’

‘Thanks. But that’s not the answer I was looking for,’ he replied.

Lynda tapped the car’s digital clock, then reached for her door. ‘Sorry to break up this love fest. But it’s almost time and the locals are about to revolt.’

TWENTY-FOUR

The nine people – bank manager, construction chiefs, and executives from corporate headquarters – shared the same hostile expression as they watched Val and Denton and Lynda pass through the open gates and approach. Like all nine were angry over the chance to make a hundred-million-dollar profit.

Bob Juniper, the site manager, greeted them with, 'By my watch, you've got just two hours and eleven minutes to perform the impossible.'

'And good morning to you too,' Denton replied.

'We won't be needing that long,' Lynda said.

'Eleven minutes should do,' Val agreed. 'Give or take.'

The eldest of the suits said, 'Mr Hayes, I'm Axel Range, head of new build at Great American Grains.'

Lynda tried and failed to stifle her smile. 'GAG? Really?'

Denton told her, 'Play nice.'

'Why should I? They're not.'

'It's their sandbox,' Denton replied. To Range, 'You were saying?'

'I have with me our head of legal and our chief financial officer. I must hereby inform you that we will hold you to the contract's strictest possible definition. Which your own people drafted.'

'That's certainly within your rights,' Denton agreed. 'Can I make sure you've cleared everyone from around the silos?'

'You've cost us a full day's work,' the site manager groused.

'For which you're earning a hundred-million-dollar profit,' Lynda cheerfully replied. 'Maybe more.'

But the executive was too wound up to stop mid-stride. 'As I was saying, if you fail to move all six silos by the hour of noon today, you forfeit the funds now residing in the escrow account, along with any and all rights you may *think* you have to the silos.'

Denton replied, 'Like I said yesterday, were that to happen, which it won't, the money and silos would be yours.'

The site manager told the others in his group, 'Don't that just beat all?'

The bank manager demanded, 'Are you some brand of federal agents?'

'No, we are not.'

The bank manager pointed to the crowd standing outside the site fence. Watching and chattering and laughing, all of them gathered by the local rumor mill, there to watch some federal nutcases get their comeuppance. He told the others, 'That's the talk in town. Feds who've been digging up dirt on people.'

Lynda laughed out loud.

The bank manager rounded on her. 'You think this is funny?'

'You'll have to excuse my associate,' Denton said. 'She doesn't get out much.'

Their response was halted by a pair of oversized vans rushing towards the entry gates. Both had folded satellite dishes adorning their roofs.

Axel Range demanded, 'Who alerted the news?'

'Not me,' Denton said. 'But I probably should have.'

The first van ignored the security guard on gate duty and pulled up close enough to the group for a woman to demand through her open window, 'Which one of you is Denton Hayes?'

'That's me.'

'Carla Weintraub, NBC News with their Fort Wayne affiliate.' She stepped out, revealing a crimson silk outfit and stiletto heels and shellacked blond hair. 'Are we too late?'

'No, no, you're right on time.'

'Our station manager got a call from Vice President Dale's campaign manager, Mr . . . Let's see, I have the name right here . . .'

A slender young man in a dress shirt and spiked hair stepped out of the second van and called over, 'Carlton Riffkind.'

The newswoman was clearly not pleased with the young man's appearance. 'Hi, Terry.'

'Carla. You're looking very red today.'

The site manager said, 'Are you seeing this?'

The bank manager told Denton, 'Mister, if you think having the press here will help you exit this mess, you're wrong.'

Val thought the young newscaster looked about sixteen. He walked over holding a wireless mike and asked, 'Can somebody tell me what's going on here?'

The construction chief said, 'Now you're talking.'

When the news anchor stuck his microphone in Bob Juniper's face, he snapped, 'Either you back off, bub, or you eat that mike.'

As the young man jumped away, the woman said, 'And he thinks it's funny to give me grief over my clothes. Every time.' She asked Denton, 'If I'm polite, would you explain why we're here?'

'Most certainly.'

She gestured to the driver of her van, who began prepping his shoulder camera. Carla pulled a mike from her purse. Terry did his best to keep Carla between him and the site manager. Carla said, 'Dale's campaign manager assured us today's event would garner national attention.'

'It will now,' Denton replied. 'Thanks to you.'

Lynda checked her watch. 'Two minutes.'

Carla asked, 'Can you give us some details on what is taking place?'

Denton pointed to Val. 'Our spokesperson will. Gladly. But we had better wait until after. Right now, you need to aim your cameras at the silos.'

Juniper told his crew, 'You ask me, this fellow just redefined crazy in the head.'

Lynda said, 'Sixty seconds.'

But their team did not arrive on time.

The camera guys had clearly shared hours waiting for a story. The two men joked quietly and shot background videos of the silos, the angry construction chiefs, the crowd beyond the fence. Then they settled their heavy shoulder gear in the vans' open rear doors. When the promised moment came and went, Carla checked her makeup in a pocket mirror, then snapped it shut loud enough to declare her irritation. Terry, the young male newscaster, called, 'What are we looking for?'

Denton merely pointed at the silos. One of the executives laughed out loud.

Another five minutes passed. Carla was pacing now, talking into her cellphone and chopping the air with her free hand. Terry sauntered over to where the cameramen sat on a van's rear ledge, spoke with them for a while, then checked his spiked hair in the side mirror.

Eight minutes. Nine.

Carla walked back, mike by her side, no longer smiling. 'How much longer is this going to take? I'm asking because I'm due to report on a *real* story back in . . .'

Lynda halted her by pointing at the sky. 'There.'

'Where?' Val squinted and searched. 'I don't see . . . . Oh.'

A tiny silvery globe appeared high overhead. It glinted in the sunlight as it drifted in from the north.

Carla cried, 'What on earth?'

Denton waved to the cameramen. 'This is your cue.'

The object flew towards them, its silent descent only heightening the crowd's consternation. Outside the fence, people began shouting. Construction workers gaped and ran about. The executives clustered together, as if finding assurance from the closeness of others that this was real, it was happening.

The silver globe approached at what to Val seemed like a leisurely pace, only it took mere seconds before it hovered directly over the six silos.

Its utter stillness contrasted sharply with the rising din from all the people gathered below. Most of whom were screaming.

Including Carla, who yelled shrilly at her cameraman, '*Scan the crowd! Scan the crowd!*'

Terry, on the other hand, just stood there, mouth agape, microphone dangling from limp fingers.

The construction chiefs shrilled high as little girls as the globe began expanding.

Val watched the crew run around, yellow hats and vests bobbing like kids in the playground as . . .

The globe completely enveloped all six silos.

There was the sound of ripping earth and the sharp bangs of snapping metal as . . .

The now gigantic silver globe lifted up, up, up, and . . .

Vanished in the clouds.

Of the silos, there was no sign.

TWENTY-FIVE

As she watched the bubble vanish beyond the clouds, Val felt it all come together. She could almost hear the questions she would not be answering, certainly not today. The old dilemmas – that of whether they were being manipulated by some alien force, or if free will still mattered, or if they were losing everything that made them humans, forming into a hive mind – all of these were framed around definitions that no longer applied. They were entering a new era. She as an individual was volunteering for what came next.

She was ready when the two stunned newscasters lifted their mikes toward Denton, and he responded with a shake of his head. Denton pointed toward Val and said, 'Ask away.'

Carla found her voice first. 'Who *are* you people?'

'My name is Valentina Garnier. I'm a journalist. I've been involved in this process since the beginning.'

Carla's wild gesture took in the entire site. '*What was that?*'

Val waited until the young man steadied his mike beside Carla's, then replied, 'We are in contact with an intelligent race on, or rather inside, the Saturn moon we know as Enceladus.'

Carla broke in with, 'But *how* do you know?'

Val liked the woman, her ability to remain focused on the key points despite everything. She was tempted to go ahead and give it to her straight. But . . .

The impression was so vivid that she might as well have seen it visually. The path of harmony. Val decided that would be how she described it in the article or book or journal, whatever. A clear way forward, coordinated with everything that was happening. The dozens of strands, more, all woven together in a path that led toward tomorrow.

Val said, 'At this point, we only know a little about this second intelligent race sharing our solar system. We know they developed around the same time as the human race, give or take a hundred thousand years.' She was aware of the nine executives and construction chiefs drawing close. One of the cameramen shifted slightly to his left, bringing them into focus as a backdrop. She heard an executive mutter something, only to be silenced by Carla hissing in their direction.

Val continued, 'The ways we use to describe or even name a race simply do not apply. For example, to call them blind suggests they once had vision and lost it. This is wrong. Their home is in a global ocean that exists beneath a mantle of ice three miles thick. There is no light in what we call the visual scale. There never has been. Which means we have no way of knowing how they look. They have no concept of visual description. Those words simply hold no meaning.'

Carla pulled the mike back and demanded, 'What does all this have to do with what we just witnessed?'

'Recently our team in England received a message that they are dying,' Val said. 'Their world's food source is almost gone. But we have only now made contact. As a result, it may be too late to save them. Just the same, we have to try.'

Carla said, 'And the silos . . .'

'We are turning them into an interplanetary transit system,' Val replied. 'My team is currently purchasing twelve thousand tons of nutrients. Our world can certainly spare them. These are all ingredients that go into the most common forms of fertilizer. Globally, we produce over a hundred thousand tons every year.'

Carla pulled back her mike, demanded, 'How is Vice President Dale involved in all this?'

'As far as I know, he isn't.'

'But his office contacted us,' Terry said, finally finding his voice.

'You'll need to ask them. Again, our group does not include the vice president.' Val started to move away.

The two newscasters cried together, 'Wait!' Then Carla asked, 'Where are you taking the silos?'

'Our base of operations is an uninhabited island in the Caribbean nation of Grenada.' Val held up her hand. 'Sorry, that's all the time I have. We depart for Enceladus in three days.'

TWENTY-SIX

Carlton placed the call mostly because he felt like it was the right thing to do. He had made numerous such moves in the past, going with his gut even when sometimes logic pointed him the opposite direction.

This was different. Totally, utterly not the same.

He was still coming to terms with how it felt to be connected on this new level. He wished there was someone he knew who was going through the same early stages. Someone with a keen interest in marking the transition. He opted to write his wife and daughter a series of emails – encrypted, of course, given the current situation. Just jotting down a few words about what he was sensing, how he felt it impacted his work and life. Today's note simply said that gut-level ideas or reactions had reached a nadir. He felt it most distinctly when he could reach out and field a new concept. Not in words. Just trying something on for size. Every time, he suddenly found himself inside a series of world-shaping events. Moving with the flow.

The energy and intensity was all there. It was not a gradual transition. He had an idea, he measured it individually, he reached out and . . . Whoosh. He was swept into the power of everything that was coming together. All the myriad of events needed to reach Enceladus on time. All the people involved. The question he asked then was always the same. Did this fit or not?

Today, the answer was unequivocal.

Carlton debated which location would be best for this call. After a moment's reflection, he decided to try to avoid the White House. Too many listening ears.

A young woman came on the line, brisk and cheerful and intelligent. She welcomed the caller to the president's re-election campaign and asked how she could help. All within a ten-second window. Carlton made a mental note to call their own central office, check on how professional and swift his team fielded calls. 'Avri Rowe, please.'

'Mr Rowe is unavailable at the moment. Is there anyone else who can help?'

'Sorry, no.'

'Who, may I ask, is calling?'

'Carlton Riffkind. Campaign manager for Terrance Dale.'

That silenced her. Then, 'Really?'

'The one and only.'

'Hold, please.'

The background music was patriotic and up-tempo. Carlton made another note to check on what his team had in place.

Then, 'Carlton?'

'Yes.'

'Olivia Estanada. Remember me?'

'Of course.' A caramel-skinned attorney with one of the sharpest minds Carlton had ever come across. 'Last time we met was . . . let's see. The DC conference on granting Washington full state status. Another lost cause.'

'You're one to speak.'

'Touché.'

'So it's really you.'

'In the flesh. Sort of.'

'What can I do for you, Carlton?'

'I was hoping to give Avri a heads-up. Professional courtesy. There's going to be a major announcement on the national evening news. I imagine it will be carried on all channels.'

'We haven't heard anything.'

'Which is why I'm calling.'

'Carlton, you've got to understand, Avri is the busiest man in town. Nobody juggles better than him, but still. Why don't you tell me and let me pass it on?'

'Sorry, Olivia. Not this time.'

'Can he call you back?'

'Sure. He's welcome to contact me any time. But this announcement goes out . . .' Carlton checked his watch. 'Twelve minutes and counting.'

'Is there a reason you waited to the very last minute?'

'The timing is awful. I agree. But I only just received word myself.'

A pause, then, 'Hold on, let me see if he can spare you a moment.'

This time the wait was much longer. Carlton walked his phone out the rear doors, circled the pool, debated whether he should go for a swim. He watched a trio of swallows write invisible script in the cloudless sky. He basked in the afternoon sun, tasted the warm breeze, felt how good it was to be alive and active and involved in something this big.

Then a deep voice barked, solid and angry as a junkyard dog. 'OK, I'm here. What.'

Not the friendliest of greetings. But still. 'I wanted to let you know—'

'I've already heard that. Talk.'

'It has to do with the group we have not yet officially mentioned.'

Silence.

'We do not at present intend to make them a part of our campaign.'

Avri demanded, 'You're calling to threaten me?'

'No, sir.' Calm. Respectful. Resolute. 'You hold all the cards. Why would I ever attempt such a thing?'

'Go on.'

'We have a breakthrough of sorts. It was picked up by a couple of regional stations. We anticipate it going out nationwide tonight.'

'Go ahead and gloat. Any momentary puff of wind in your direction won't help, and you know it.'

Carlton shook his head to the sky. The man really was insufferable. 'If I could please have the number to your cellphone, I will send you the raw footage.'

'Does Dale know you've made this call?'

'He does.'

'So he's involved in this charade. I knew it.'

'Sir, Avri, this is as far from charade as you can possibly get. May I have your number?'

Another momentary silence, then Avri read off the number. Barked, really. And cut the connection.

Carlton linked the video feed to the number, sent it off. He said to the sky overhead, 'It really has been a pleasure to mess with your day.'

TWENTY-SEVEN

Six thirty that evening Kelly ran the nearly empty Pentagon City streets, reveling in the rain and the faceless man-made canyons. Ninety minutes earlier, the streets had been teeming with late-model cars and SUVs. But the pedestrian traffic never picked up much. All day long, people slipped from their buildings, bought a meal or coffee, smoked cigarettes, then slipped back inside. The sidewalks were broad and clean, the streets well paved. But the employees of these modern buildings were mostly trained to go unseen. They never spoke to strangers. They kept their professional masks in place, especially in public. Even when their work wasn't secret in any way. To confess they merely pushed federal paper reduced them in their own eyes. Many of the people employed in Pentagon City worked for defense or one of the intelligence agencies. These simple bureaucrats knew the person next in line at the sandwich shop might be returning from some place where burnt cordite spiced the dry wind. Where life was lived one breath at a time.

She had been the first to move into the apartments inside their new headquarters. She took one of the two penthouses because it was expected. All the housing units were identical. The view from the eleventh floor was pretty much the same as the ones below: a bit more sunlight, a few more rooftops. Kelly liked it because the place was as close to sanitized as she could get. It held no trace of memories. Nothing could be done about the sorrow and aching void, but her nights were calmer, her sleep relatively undisturbed. Even now that she had stopped using the pills.

The rain lashed her as she ran, carried by a southeast wind that pushed hard every time she emerged at a crosswalk. Tires of passing cars sounded sibilant as they pushed through the rushing water. Her footsteps were liquid cymbals.

As usual, she stopped in front of their building and used the bike rack as a stretch bar. The rain streaking her body and face was simply part of the day. That done, she stepped to the right-hand glass door and waved. The agent on guard detail buzzed her inside. Kelly only used members of her team on the front-door detail. The last thing she wanted, the very last, was to rely on outsiders to keep them secure. They all served their time on the duty roster.

One of Rabbit's original team was handling security. She greeted Kelly with, 'Are you seeing this?' As soon as the door clicked shut, the young woman's gaze returned to the tablet propped on the desk below the counter's ledge. Her eyes on the unseen screen, the woman added, 'Darren said to let him know when you got back.'

'Tell him to come on up, let himself into the apartment, put on a fresh pot.' She continued toward the elevator. Whatever it was, Kelly did not want to hear it piecemeal from a woman not trained in handling raw intel. She assumed it had to do with the vice president. That afternoon, she had heard from Agnes that the president's team had almost decided the VP was going to be forced to resign. Kelly thought that played into their opponents' hands, and said so. But too many people with voices that mattered felt otherwise. Their endless debate left her tired.

Midway through her shower, Kelly found herself recalling her first contact with Agnes Pendalon. The woman had brought Kelly's team and Rabbit together for a midnight run across the border. Their stated goal was to infiltrate a heavily guarded compound run by the latest Mexican drug lord and human trafficker. Subdue the bad guys. Bring back all of the would-be migrants that Rabbit identified.

Kelly had leaped at the chance. After all, the gang was led by the man responsible for her fiancé's murder.

Then, upon their return from a successful operation, Agnes Pendalon had dropped the bombshell.

The gang's sudden rise to power had been fueled by a new and elevated level of human connection or communication. Here was the point where so many traditional definitions needed to be refined or tossed out altogether.

This new connection had arrived by way of an unknown alien source.

Alien as in, well, alien.

One masquerading as a rowan tree.

In the days that followed, as Kelly and her new team pushed hard on their California-based investigation, she had often wondered how Agnes Pendalon had chosen her. After all, she and her team were less than two years out of agent training, still serving in relatively menial positions. But Kelly had been assigned team leader, she assumed because of her loss. Because this made their mission personal.

These recollections brought her back with riveting force to the issue Vivienne had raised earlier today. The one question Kelly had never bothered to ask was: *what if*.

What if Agnes Pendalon had decided long before contacting Kelly that everyone who had accepted the alien's so-called gift was an enemy?

What if she was wrong?

What if Agnes had identified in Kelly an individual so wounded by her fiancé's death that she would take aim at anyone even remotely connected to this new group?

What if Agnes was wrong to assume they were, in fact, the enemy?

What if Kelly's desperate need for revenge had blinded her? What if that was the reason for Agnes appointing her team leader? What if Agnes had gone searching for someone who would not question whether this group were all enemies? All tainted by the drug lord's murderous brush?

What if they and their mission had it wrong?

In all the time they had worked together, through everything Kelly and her team had endured, she had never once thought to ask these questions. The risk in not asking was clear enough: what if she was being played?

Kelly emerged from the bedroom rubbing a hand towel through her hair and still working on that final thought. How it all came down to motive. Then she noticed how her living room did not welcome her with the requested smell of fresh-brewed coffee. Despite the fact that Rabbit and Darren were standing there.

Waiting for her. Sharing the same grim expression. 'What's going on?'

'We're not exactly sure,' Darren replied.

'We know enough,' Rabbit said. 'We just don't want to accept it.'

Darren nodded agreement. 'We also have no idea what it means.'

She set the towel on the kitchenette's granite countertop. 'What are we talking about here?'

'The nightly news carried this story as a probable joke,' Darren said. 'Which is why we didn't bother you. It was vaguely absurd to begin with, and the newscasters added to this by calling it a possible prank.'

'Then the twenty-four-hour news channels started in,' Rabbit said. 'And the more we hear, the more we're fairly certain it's not a prank at all.'

Darren nodded, clearly angered by the need to say, 'We now think it's real.'

'It's them,' Rabbit said. 'Has to be.'

Kelly settled on a counter stool. Readied herself. 'Show me.'

Rabbit touched the controls. As soon as the screen lit up, he started scrolling. Ten seconds to each channel. Fox, CNN, MSNBC, Al Jazeera, Spanish, BBC – everyone was talking about it now. Long before the actual image was replayed, Kelly knew they were right. This was real. It had happened. The genie was out of the box.

She watched as the silvery illuminated globe swallowed the silos, then lifted into the sky and vanished, leaving a gaping space in the middle of the new agricultural compound. She listened as Valentina Garnier explained what was happening. She watched the talking heads bring in an astronomer and flash up an image of the Saturn moon Enceladus. The most recent satellite photos showed spumes of frozen water vapor blowing miles into the starlit sky. Kelly said, 'Find another channel showing the silos.'

She watched it all again. Then, 'Have our people checked this out?'

Darren replied, 'NSA has a military transport inbound with the actual tapes. But their first assessment is, yeah, it's genuine.'

She asked Rabbit, 'Anything from your team?'

He sketched a design with both hands, which was Rabbit's way of searching for terms that didn't exist. Yet. 'We're still cut off from telepaths that are not part of our team. Just the same, my group is convinced this is a real event.'

'All of your new team who are connected, they feel this way?'

He nodded. 'It's unanimous. Without any doubt or hesitation.'

Darren said, 'Agnes has called for a debriefing. Ninety minutes. Which probably means they're waiting for confirmation from NSA before raising the red flag.'

Kelly's phone rang. She checked the readout, said, 'I don't believe this.'

The two men said together, 'What!'

She hit the connection, put it on speaker, said, 'Barry, is it really you?'

'In the flesh,' he replied. 'We're out. Sort of.'

This time she shared her team members' gaping astonishment. 'What exactly does that mean, out?'

'I'm instructed to tell you we're being shifted to an Ottawa airport motel.' Barry's voice was as flat as pounded tin. 'Restricted to our rooms. Meals courtesy of Uber. Which is a huge improvement, believe me.'

'When can you come home?'

'No idea.' Barry sounded exhausted. Shattered. 'We've been told this is a conditional release.'

'Which means what?'

'My question exactly,' he replied. 'When I know, you know.' A voice spoke in the background. Harsh, barking. 'They're grabbing my phone. Call our families, let them know—'

The line went dead.

Kelly sat there. Thinking.

Finally, Rabbit asked, 'What just happened?'

Darren said, 'They don't need our team anymore.'

Rabbit stared at him.

'Think about it. What was Barry's incarceration all about? We all agreed they were being held as hostages. Why? The answer's clear enough. Leverage. Keeping us in line. Forcing us to face the new reality.' He gestured at the blank television screen. 'But it's all changed now.'

Kelly rose from her seat. Straightened her back. Wishing she had time for another run. Go out and do her best to race away from the confusion and the unsettling fear that everything was now out of their control. 'Ready the team. We meet in thirty.'

Rabbit showed confusion. 'I'm still not clear on what is going on here.'

'Darren is right,' Kelly said. 'This changes everything.'

TWENTY-EIGHT

Val's team flew straight from Iowa to Los Angeles. Their private jet landed at Van Nuys FBO in the late afternoon. A black Escalade limo was there to sweep them westwards, compliments of Connor, who according to Denton had been working the phones nonstop since their second task had been assigned.

Their hotel was the Maybourne Beverly Hills on Canon. Connor Breach was standing outside the hotel entrance when they pulled up. She greeted Denton with affectionate heat. Val did her best to be happy for them and what they shared.

Connor greeted Val with a second-tier embrace, shook Lynda's hand, confirmed she had checked them all in, and said their meeting was set up for nine the next morning. She handed Val a new credit card along with her room key and said, 'I hope you won't take this the wrong way, but you need to look the part. And that's going to require some work.'

They all had junior suites overlooking the Beverly Çanon Gardens. Val opened the balcony doors before showering off the journey, the morning, the night before. Or at least trying. She dressed in her least wrinkled outfit and returned downstairs to find Lynda standing by the front entrance, watching a pair of Ferraris leave the front courtyard in a loud display of power. She greeted Val with, 'Girl's got to hang her hat somewhere, I suppose.'

They walked the four blocks down to the Beverly Wiltshire, then made a slow and steady procession up Rodeo Drive, collecting bags along the way. They stopped for an early dinner at the Urasawa, reveling in the rare gift of a night with no greater responsibility than spending money.

Half past eight the next morning, they met on the hotel's rooftop terrace. Val was dressed in new Versace slacks that managed to somehow appear both conservative and alluring. Ditto for her NicoBlu high-collared blouse of Shantung silk. Chalk-blue Ferragamo pumps. Connor kissed her cheek and said, 'You go, girl.'

'Cartier was singing my song,' Val replied. 'I resisted.'

Their very own waiter hovered by a linen-draped table, shaded from the rising sun by a square awning only slightly smaller than a circus tent. The hotel's breakfast room was on the ground floor. Officially, the rooftop restaurant did not open until noon. But for a Beverly Hills-sized surcharge it was possible to reserve a private space. Only one other table was occupied, separated from them by the sweep-around bar. A Hollywood star was meeting seven studio types who hung on her every word. Lynda draped the jacket of her new executive-style suit over the back of a chair so that she faced away from the other group. 'Doesn't pay for your security to be all gah-gah over the table candy.'

Denton ordered coffee and fresh juice for everyone, then asked Val, 'Everything OK?'

She seated herself and weaved her head from side to side. 'I'm not sure.'

'Do you need something?'

When Val did not respond, Lynda said, 'The lady will be fine when it matters.'

In truth, Val was very glad to be playing a supporting role that morning. Her night had been strangely unsettling. She had slept well, but three times she'd woken from dreams that had her shooting out into deep space, lured into an impossible journey by messages that rendered her baffled and frightened both. Each time, she was almost gentled back to sleep by the same wordless communication. Not a song, no melody, but carrying the same sort of soothing calm. When she woke, as she ate her room-service breakfast and prepared for the day ahead, she was carried forward by that same impossible balance. On the one hand, she was a day closer to leaving Earth, possibly forever. On the other, her heart and mind was linked to a tune without music.

Calm and frightened in equal measure.

The realtors showed up early, a sternly cheerful silver-haired woman and her aide. The silver-haired lady introduced herself as Stella Reed, then mentioned the young man's name in a manner that suggested none of them needed to remember it. Stella had a linebacker's jaw, crystal green eyes, and an outfit that defined elegant attire. She and her young associate declined coffee, asked about their hotel rooms, complimented the weather. Then Stella said, 'Your attorney Ms Breach informs us your house requirements are rather urgent.'

Connor replied, 'Our needs could not be more time-critical.' She passed over a sheet with three printed addresses. 'We are interested in these properties.'

The realtor frowned as she accepted the page. 'Yesterday you stated you were uncertain which homes fit your requirements.'

'Our associates only completed their initial research this morning,' Connor replied.

Denton asked, 'Are they still for sale?'

Stella handed the page to her aide, who got busy on his phone. The young man confirmed, 'As of today, all three are available.'

Two were located in Beverly Hills, the other in Bel Air. The realtor said, 'All of these are excellent properties. Two I personally represent. The other residence I have shown twice. Any of them will make a truly outstanding residence.'

Denton said, 'We want to acquire all three.'

That stopped her.

Denton continued, 'We are hereby offering fifty percent above your current asking prices. But only if we can finalize the purchases by close of business today.'

The young man laughed out loud.

Connor added, 'Anything the owners do not wish to have included in the sale must be removed by six this afternoon.'

'Otherwise, we will be forced to take our business elsewhere,' Denton said. 'Everything related to timing is non-negotiable.'

Connor said, 'Acquiring all three properties brings the total to eighty-seven million dollars. Am I correct in assuming an initial down payment of five percent would secure these estates?'

Stella managed, 'Well, certainly, I suppose . . .'

'Excellent.' Connor passed over an unsealed envelope. 'Here is a banker's draft for four point five million.'

The young man watched his boss open the envelope and draw out the check with unsteady fingers. He asked, 'Don't you even want to view the homes?'

'Most certainly,' Denton replied. 'Once we have an agreement in principle, have opened an escrow account for the full purchase prices, and you have started moving these sales forward.'

TWENTY-NINE

Kelly sat in one of three Barcaloungers in Nathan's parents' den. The last time she had visited, there had only been two of the fold-out easy chairs. As always, Kelly had refused to take the second whenever Martha, Nathan's mother, was anywhere close. The two stubborn women often wound up sitting together on the sofa, with the lounger left empty. Now there were three.

Kelly's was so comfortable she could have easily curled up catlike and dozed. Except for two items. The first was that she had returned on this particular day because it was the second anniversary of Nathan's murder. As soon as Kelly arrived, they had gone straight to Nathan's grave. Since then, they had not spoken his name or uttered a word about their son. Kelly's fiancé. The one love of her lonely life. There was no need. Nathan's absence surrounded them all.

The second reason was what dominated the news channels. Twenty-four seven. It even pushed the coming primaries off the air.

Jerry, Nathan's father, said, 'That inbound bubble is probably the one from Durban.' He flipped handwritten pages on the clipboard in his lap. 'Two thousand tons of potassium chloride fertilizer, according to the South African news feed.'

Their home stood southeast of Roanoke, Virginia. The property covered a rise near the Mill Mountain Trailhead and overlooked the Roanoke River and the forests beyond. A few of the maples were just beginning to show off their autumn finery. In another month, the trees would look like living flames. Nathan had always thought his hometown represented the finest elements of life in America.

Jerry made notes on a fresh sheet, collating as he spoke. 'That makes four thousand tons of potassium and two of nitrogen fertilizer. A fourth silo is filled with micronutrients – boron, chlorine, copper, iron, manganese, molybdenum, zinc, some soluble sulfates. According to my research and what the pundits are saying, all this is contained in standard high-grade field enrichments systems.' He set the clipboard on his side table. 'I suppose you could go to a lot of trouble and mix up a low-yield explosion. But what's the point?'

The den was floored and wainscoted in pecky cypress that Nathan and his dad had harvested and milled and set in place using wooden pegs. The home was filled with aromas of Nathan's favorite meal: white bean casserole and home-smoked chicken and cornbread and coleslaw spiced with cream of horseradish. It was as fine a setting as Kelly could have imagined for missing the man and watching her world be redefined.

As the globe descended, Jerry asked, 'Is it true what they're saying, you can't track them on radar?'

'Once they're airborne and underway, we lose all contact until we regain visual,' Kelly confirmed. 'Their flight pattern takes them around thirty miles high. They rise straight up, level off, then bang and gone. Sound barrier is broken in seconds. NSA estimates acceleration is somewhere around eight gravities.'

'Any idea how they do this?'

'None. We assume they've had a land-based version in operation up in northern Canada. An entire city-sized region that's completely impenetrable. We're still no clearer on how it operates.'

'Here we go.' Jerry leaned forward as the arriving globe touched the Grenada island's shield. There was a smooth joining of the two forces. 'I can't tell if that top bubble dissolves or if the bottom one reaches up and swallows it.'

'NSA is pretty sure they merge,' Kelly said.

'I guess they should know.' They watched in silence as the bubbles joined, then Jerry asked, 'What's next?'

'Two more inbound shipments.' Kelly lifted her phone and checked the feed from Darren. 'Alberta, a potassium mine up close to the Northwest Territories. Then two thousand tons of nitrate inbound from a mine outside Melbourne, Australia.'

Jerry was a retired Marine colonel, still lean and clear-eyed and precise in his sixty-ninth year. 'What do your superiors think of all this?'

By superiors, Kelly knew, Jerry meant the current administration. 'It's a madhouse.'

'I can imagine.'

'Everybody shouting, pointing fingers, no idea how to respond, nothing else getting done. Avri is desperately trying to reshape the president's re-election campaign around everything that's happening. The only thing Avri hates more than uncertainty is when events move beyond his control. He's in a perpetual rage. His team are like a hutch of frightened rabbits.'

Jerry grunted. 'Your new opponent certainly isn't helping any.'

Kelly assumed he wasn't speaking about the opposing party's candidate. 'Dale is definitely part of the problem.'

Terrance Dale was naturally fielding questions about these developments at every stop. He handled the issue with the ease of a lifetime spent in the political arena. He repeatedly told the press that he'd always been a fierce promoter of private enterprise, including newcomers to the space field. America needed to remain at the forefront of world-changing innovation. No, he had not been in direct contact with anyone involved in this project. But he wanted them to know that they were welcome in the nation he intended to both lead and promote.

The man's words sent both the president and his campaign manager into almost uncontrollable fury.

Jerry said, 'Times like this, a little distance from ground zero can help.' He glanced over. 'We're always glad to see you, Kelly. I hope you know that.'

She forced herself to say the words. 'This is the only real home I have.'

Martha reached over from the third chair and gripped Kelly's hand. She was by nature a calm force, the glue that held this family's tattered remnants in place. 'You could not be more of a daughter if I had birthed you myself. I don't know how to say it any plainer.'

They remained like that, bound by forces stronger than what they witnessed on the screen, until Martha asked, 'Did they just drop the shield around the island?'

'Not exactly,' Kelly said, wiping her eyes. 'Watch the news chopper doing another sweep. OK, checkout the top right of the screen . . . see it?'

'Like a wavy distortion,' Martha said.

'NASA thinks the shield or whatever it is has entered a different state,' Kelly said. 'There has to be a reason. Becoming transparent may require less energy. Something.'

A timer pinged. The three of them all rose together and entered the kitchen. Moving together with smoothness and ease. Like a family. Filling plates and glasses, shifting the dining table slightly so they could all still see the wall-mounted screen. Seating themselves, holding hands, Martha and Kelly seated to either side of Jerry, the two women doing what they always did and reaching out to the empty space. A brief gesture, just long enough to connect with the fractured past. Silenced by shared sorrow, doing their best to push the internal reset button. Finally, Kelly managed to say, 'This is delicious.'

They did not speak again until the meal was finished and the table cleared and a fresh pot of coffee brewing. They elected to remain there at the table, anchored by one another's closeness, the hardwood chairs, the late-afternoon light suggesting a clarity of vision none of them felt.

Jerry continued shifting from one channel to the next, then halted when a news helicopter rose and backed away far enough to show a bird's-eye view of the entire vista. The island was an unattractive mound with no beach to speak of, possibly volcanic, mostly bare rock blanketed with scrub and guano. The globe surrounding the island and six silos remained transparent, showing the structure resting upon a flattened ridge at the island's center.

The surrounding ocean was crammed with every imaginable form of boat, from luxury cruisers to military craft to jet skis. Hundreds of them. The news channel's view shifted to sea level, showing a yacht filled with bikini-clad partiers, drinks in one hand, phones in the other, shooting selfies.

'Idiots,' Martha said.

'They're not alone,' Jerry said. 'Check out that boat screen's top left.'

Kelly watched as the news camera refocused on a speedboat accelerating directly at the island. As they passed one boat after another, hundreds of revelers cheered them on.

'Stupid and stoned and on holiday,' Martha said. 'Dreadful combination.'

The boat collided with an invisible barrier or fence – something. It yawed forward about ten feet, slow enough not to obliterate the craft, but the deceleration still threw everyone around. At the same time, they began jerking like marionettes as the craft became surrounded by a sparking electric field.

Jerry said, 'A while before you got here, a news chopper flew too close. Afterwards, they said it felt like they were hit by a giant Taser. All the electrics went dead, but the chopper didn't fall. It just hung there, caught in midair, until the engines restarted. Craziest thing you ever saw.'

'That's the word I was searching for,' Martha said. 'Crazy.'

'I saw it before I left Pentagon City,' Kelly replied. 'Defense has no idea how they're pulling it off.'

They watched the speedboat drift away, engines dead. The craft's occupants picked themselves up and staggered about. The news camera zeroed in on two women screaming in fear or pain or both.

Martha asked, 'Should we be afraid?'

Jerry nodded at the screen. 'That's the question, sure enough.'

Kelly felt safe enough here in this place to release the dilemma that had plagued her ever since leaving the therapist's office. 'Are they the enemy?'

Jerry nodded again. 'What do your superiors say?'

Kelly did not respond.

He accepted her silence with a third nod. Up and down, a sharp acknowledgment. Not looking her way as he said, 'The military has always been worried when there's a chance politicians mix up that word, enemy, with one that is closer to the truth.'

'Opponent,' Kelly said. She and Jerry and their late son had discussed this any number of times. 'Nathan always said, viewing citizens with opposing views as the enemy forms a crisis point for democracy.'

He rewarded her with a smile. 'He learned that from me.'

'But a number of my superiors are former military,' Kelly said. 'Agnes Pendalon and General Skarren are both convinced that group represents an existential threat to our nation's future. This view is shared by everyone inside the White House. And many others inside the intelligence communities.'

Jerry was silent as yet another luminescent bubble descended from the clouds. The shield encircling the silos went opaque and grew to where the smaller object was consumed. Absorbed. Something. 'Where did that shipment originate?'

Kelly reached for her phone and checked the feed from Darren. 'Canada.'

He addressed his words to the screen. 'You know as well as I do, our military doesn't follow lockstep behind any single line of thought.'

'You're saying, you don't agree with the Pentagon's view of events?' She caught herself, changed it to, 'With us?'

'If I was still on active duty, I would tell you that I'll follow orders and trust my superiors to decide what is best for America.'

'But you're not a serving Marine,' she replied. 'What do you say now?'

Jerry replied in a manner suggesting he had thought long and hard on this very issue. 'An enemy combatant is defined as someone who through his or her actions endangers the United States and its citizens. They engage in hostilities on behalf of a group or nation deemed to be a direct threat.' He pointed at the screen. 'There is nothing I see in any of their actions that fits that definition.'

'All this is the result of an alien's infestation of our people,' Kelly said. Not disagreeing. Rather, she laid out the arguments that had so impacted her and her team. 'If we don't stop them now, we're lost.'

'That is certainly a risk.' He turned around. Stared at her with the calm and steady gaze of a man who had sent his troops into peril. 'And they may well be right.'

'Finish that thought,' Kelly said.

'Are you certain?'

'I need to hear this,' she said.

'Very well. These days, our leaders tend to see any opposition as the enemy. Any threat to their power structure is defined as a danger to our nation. At best, that perspective risks clouding their judgment. At worst, it represents a mortal threat to democracy. Why? Because their personal ambitions are not the same as our nation's future. Our only hope lies in leaders who accept the challenge of looking beyond their own self-interests. And those of their followers. And acknowledge their so-called opponents may not actually be in the wrong.' Jerry watched the main bubble become translucent once more. 'We're facing a point of great change, no question about that. I just hope there's a leader out there able and willing to face the challenge . . .'

Jerry's words were cut short by Kelly's phone. She had programmed a special ringtone to be activated in an emergency. When she answered, Darren reported, 'Barry and his team just landed at Dulles. They're being held by security. No surprise, since none of them carried passports or ID.'

Kelly was already up and moving. She rushed into her bedroom and started jamming her belongings into the carryall. 'I'm leaving for Dulles now.'

'We'll meet you there. Grey Mathers and Rabbit are with me. Agnes is tied up at the White House, says she'll join us here for the debrief.'

'Call me with any updates.' Kelly rushed back into the den and announced, 'I have to go.'

THIRTY

As the realtors shifted to another table and began working their phones, Val studied her three friends. Denton, Connor, and Lynda were focused on Connor's phone, watching as online news feeds showed the silvery globes descending from the Caribbean sky.

Finally, Val said, 'There's something we need to discuss.'

Denton looked up long enough to ask, 'Can it wait?'

'Actually, no.'

Reluctantly, Connor cut off her phone, asked, 'Should we go back to our room?'

'Here is fine.' Val reached into her purse for her own phone, set it on the table. 'Up to now, we have never talked about our individual experiences of the crop circle events.'

Denton pointed to the realtors. 'Is there a particular reason why this can't wait until we're done spending money?'

This time, it was Lynda who replied, 'Apparently, there is, Denton. Otherwise, the lady wouldn't be asking.'

Val went on, 'We carry different perspectives, and we need to learn from them. Denton and Connor in New York, Lynda and me in the crop circle.'

'It felt to me like the distance between us was chopped to inches by that communication with Saturn's moon,' Connor said.

'See, that's what I'm talking about.' Val turned on her phone, checked the battery level, then started recording. 'There has to be parameters to what we say. Boundaries are important in any interview, but especially when dealing with a highly emotional event. The sheer amount of incoming data has to be confined. Only then can it be expressed in a way that other people can understand. And share in the experience.'

Connor said, 'That right there is why you're serving as our official record keeper.'

'One by one,' Val said. 'Your first impression, your clearest and most vivid memory of what happened when we made contact. And no interruptions. Who goes first?'

'I will,' Connor said, her response immediate. As if she had been thinking about it for days. Wishing for a chance to express it aloud. 'One minute I was busy working through a ream of documents with Consuela Almeida. She's the junior attorney who joined with us at the Grenadian Consulate. Suddenly, between one breath and the next, I was struck by the first big bang.'

'The stone circle,' Denton offered, earning a glare from everyone. 'Sorry.'

'It felt like the world's biggest alarm clock,' Connor recalled. 'Right then, I became reconnected. More intensely than ever before. I had to stop working through my own reactions because Consuela was suddenly faced with an entirely new level of experiences and was on the verge of freaking out.'

Val pulled out pad and pen, began making tight one-word notes. Points where she needed to go back and study, elements that would form the next chapter's spine. Marking the time-point on her phone's recorder. Anchoring herself in the process. She said, 'The background is both beautiful and helpful. Now let's move to the issue. Your first impression of the event itself.'

'I was in an arena,' Connor replied, her gaze distant. 'So big it held all of us. From everywhere. And down there at ground zero, I observed an old soul. A gentle spirit. In a very weak state. Frail. So close to death that after it indeed I thought maybe I misread the contact. And the communication. As if it had not come and asked for help. Rather, it was there to greet us and say farewell. All at the same time.'

Lynda covered her eyes.

'OK, good,' Val said. 'Who's next?'

'I'll go,' Denton said. 'Soon as that first event rejoined us, I searched for Connor. I've spent so many nights wondering what it would be like to love with the connection fully there.' He stopped. Swallowed hard. 'I touched her heart. It almost broke me.'

Val watched Connor lean in, offer strength and comfort and more beside. Val did her best to move beyond the blooming ache. 'And then?'

Denton kept hold of Connor's hand with both of his. 'That emotion, that intensity, shaped how I saw the next event. At least, that's how it felt. They had been waiting for this moment, when we managed to move beyond the chrysalis and connect. They had feared it wouldn't come in time. Their gratitude for us listening, being there for them, just tore me apart.'

Connor saw the younger realtor rise from their table and look their way, phone in hand. She called over, 'We need a few moments.'

The realtor waved his phone. 'But we're ready to move forward . . .'

'That's just dandy. I'll tell you when *we* are ready.' Connor turned back and told Lynda, 'Now you.'

She launched straight in. 'They had one voice. Not a unified voice representing many. One unique spokesperson. My impression was they made that happen by a single entity separating itself from all the others. Accomplishing this was extremely difficult. They don't think in numbers. Or individually. They were trying to interpret and communicate in a way so we could comfortably connect with them. Which meant this individual split apart. Became a solitary unit.'

Val liked how they all needed time for a long breath. Taking the concept in deep. She liked that a lot. They remained silent and communing until Denton asked, 'What about you, Val?'

'My impression of the event is deeply imbedded in what I've been experiencing ever since. Like I think on that moment, and bind that to the *now,* and I see a different *then.*' She gave them a chance to question, show confusion, something. Instead, they simply watched, studied, absorbed. She liked that sense of unquestioning unity. So much. 'Every night since then, I wake up at least once and feel terrified by what's about to happen. Within a few minutes – less – I experience this overwhelming message of gratitude. Inside the communication there is an underlay. Like the only way I can truly understand their message, their gift, is to learn something else.'

Connor asked, 'Which is?'

'That for them, time isn't linear. If I'm correctly understanding their message, they're not just grateful because we're willing to try and help. It's more like they already know we're successful. They're already aware that they're OK. Our arrival, this transfer of nutrients, is already growing food. They're going to survive.' It was her turn to swallow hard. 'We've made our first interplanetary friends. For as long as our two races live. They are with us, whatever comes.'

THIRTY-ONE

They did not finish inspecting the three homes and signing the final documents until a few minutes after seven. There was no real reason for them to be as exhausted as they all clearly felt. After all, the realtors and their minions had done the heavy lifting. They stood and waited while sweating movers carted away the final items from their third home, did the quickest walk-through in history, accepted keys and codes, and departed. No one even suggested they stay overnight in one of their new dwellings, which was at least a little strange, given how the places were beyond move-in ready. Other than a few gaps on walls where valuable paintings once hung, some bare spots on floors now missing Persian carpets, a few empty stands for antique vases and statues, the places came fully loaded. Right down to designer silk sheets and bottles of vintage wine they might pour into stemmed crystal.

They stopped by a Asian-fusion food van that had been Connor's favorite while she called LA home. As they waited for their order, Connor kissed Denton's cheek and said, 'Thanks for going all out tonight.' When he showed utter confusion, she tapped her wedding ring. 'One year today.'

The guy behind the counter said, 'Man, you better hope the lady's not armed.'

Lynda told Connor, 'My piece is back in the room, if you care to wait.'

The counter-guy pointed out behind Denton. 'The hills are that-away.'

A smiling cook set their order on the counter and told Connor, 'I keep a knife extra sharp for times just like this.'

'She ain't kidding,' the guy said. 'You best run while you still got legs.'

Denton backed away. 'I've just lost my appetite.'

Connor grabbed his arm and hauled him back. 'Sweetie pie, I'll remember this anniversary for the rest of my days.'

'And not in a good way,' the guy said. 'Enjoy your last meal.'

Val stood to one side, smiling and sad in equal measure. As they carried trays to a neighboring park table, her phone rang. She checked the readout and said, 'It's Chakkan.'

The Thai engineer greeted her with, 'How's life in the big city?'

'Denton forgot it was their first wedding anniversary.'

The young man loved having a reason to laugh. 'There's a floor in Bali with his name on it.'

She set the phone on the table and hit the speaker button. 'What time is it over there?'

'Two the next afternoon, relative to LA.'

'OK, that's confusing.'

'Tell me. Which is why I went for something simple, like electrical engineering.'

'That's what I've always heard,' Val replied. 'MIT, home to simple minds.'

'Back to the matter at hand. Have all the sales gone through?'

'We've made some realtors and former homeowners very happy.'

'Have you seen them?'

'These are some awesome houses.'

'Is one gated?'

'All three are.'

'Better and better. We're after the one that's most secluded. Nothing visible from the street. A big lawn would help.'

That did not require thought. 'The Bel Air place. Almost an acre of parkland. Surrounded by hedges big as mountains.'

'Outstanding,' Chakkan said. 'We'll see you at four tomorrow morning. Your time.'

Val exchanged looks with the others. 'Is that a joke?'

'Tick tock, remember? Not to mention how we'd rather show up when the city's snoozing. Are the longitudinal coordinates Connor sent us correct?'

Connor leaned forward. 'I checked when on site. All three are spot on.'

'Great. Somebody please be there to lay out the welcome mat. Bye now.'

Val cut the connection. 'Given as how it's your anniversary, I volunteer to cut my night short.'

'Our night,' Lynda corrected.

'Given as how it's our anniversary,' Connor said, planting a sweet-and-sour spiced kiss on Denton's cheek, 'we accept.'

At three thirty-five in the morning, Val and Lynda pulled up to the Bel Air estate's main gates. Lynda rose from their rented Buick and asked, 'What was that code again?'

Val checked the contract, replied, 'Triple seven, triple nine.'

She punched the numbers into the security keypad and watched the gates swing open. 'Check this out.'

Val watched as ankle-height lights flickered on, illuminating the circular drive. A central fountain came to life, strobes coloring the musical water. When Lynda slipped back behind the wheel, she said, 'Billionaires get the best toys.'

A pair of gas flames now flanked the pillared entryway. More lights formed artistic designs around flower beds and decorative palms. Others rimmed the broad swath of lawn. Lynda pulled around so the car faced the exit and said, 'Go close the gates; I'll open the house for our arriving guests.'

But as Val approached the gates, two young men stepped from the shadows. She was about to scream for backup when one called, 'Valentina Garnier?'

'It's just Val.'

'Chakkan told us to meet him.' He glanced worriedly at the house. 'Is this really the right place?'

'Be it ever so humble.' She waved them inside and coded the interior gate-pad. 'And you are?'

'Raja Singh. My friend is Charlie Durrant. We're postdocs in applied physics at UCLA.'

'Or we were,' his friend said. 'Day after tomorrow, we're apparently becoming astronauts.'

Lynda appeared in the front doorway and called, 'I don't recall hearing anything about house guests.'

'Lynda, meet Doctors Durrant and Singh,' Val replied. 'Apparently, they're supposed to be here.'

'I guess that works.' She descended the stairs, greeted the

newcomers, and told Val, 'Same code for the house, the windows, both gates, pool house, garages. Either the realtors made the change for the sake of showing the home or the former owners had an infantile take on security.'

'That won't be our problem for long.'

'No, guess not.' Lynda studied her.

'What?'

She shrugged. 'Just wondering how it was for you, watching Denton and Connor.'

Val did not ask what she was talking about. 'I miss him.'

'I know you do.'

'So much.' A hard breath. 'Watching the two of them changes nothing. But it does. Like he should have been here and part of this.'

'I'm here for you,' Lynda said. 'Just so you know.'

A shout from the two men turned them both around. Val followed their outstretched arms to where a new star had appeared. 'Looks like our mystery guests are arriving.'

The silver globe descended impossibly fast, the light soft as moonlight at first. It strengthened steadily until a globe hovered overhead, only slightly smaller than the house. It shifted to the lawn's precise center, lowered, and faded away.

A single dog barked, then went quiet. Otherwise, the only sounds were the tinkling fountain and a bird's musical complaint over having been woken too early.

There in front of them stood an Indonesian-style thatched hut. On stilts, no less. The walls were woven palm fronds, the roof made from thick coconut fiber. The screened windows held no glass. The shutters were hinged at the top and held open by wooden planks. Light streamed through the windows and every crack and crevice in the woven walls.

Chakkan flung open the door and called, '*Mi casa, su casa!*'

A voice from inside the hut shrilled, 'Out of my way!'

Chakkan stepped aside. Elizabeth Larkin, astrophysicist and professor of theoretical physics, emerged carrying a double handful of electronic gear. She stomped across the stubby porch, descended the raw-plank floors, and glared at Val. 'Is it true what they're saying? You've agreed to go on this *idiotic* mission?'

'Wouldn't miss it for the world,' Val assured her. 'Bad joke.'

Elizabeth spotted the two young men. 'Durrant, right? And Singh? I can't believe you've volunteered to throw your lives away.' She shifted her load, yelled, 'You're all going to die! I hope you know that!'

Chakkan re-emerged with his own load. 'Born to moan, this one.'

Elizabeth glared at Chakkan. 'Just because he managed to fly us here in thirty minutes, you actually think you'll survive this *insanity*?'

Val asked Chakkan, 'You crossed the Pacific in half an hour?'

Sandra Carroll, former associate professor of mathematics at UPenn, was the next to emerge. 'It would have been a lot faster if Beth hadn't complained about speed limits.'

'Sound barriers,' Chakkan corrected.

'Same thing. Hi, Val. How are you holding up?'

'Depends on the hour,' Val replied. 'Excited and terrified in equal measure. How about you?'

'I have my moments.'

Elizabeth started toward the house, still berating the two wide-eyed young men. 'You're *crazy* if you think that crew can safely take you *a billion miles*.'

'Actually,' Val said, 'it's two.'

Elizabeth glanced back, like she was struggling to remember who Val was.

'Two billion,' Val said. 'Return journey, remember?'

Elizabeth snorted and marched for the house. 'Soon as I align this equipment, I am *out of here*.'

'She's been that way the entire trip,' Sandra said. 'Care to give us a hand?'

'Sure thing.'

But as she started up the hut's wooden stairs, Lynda said, 'One second.' When she had all their attention, she said, 'Just so everybody's clear on this point. I'm going.'

To her surprise, Chakkan turned her way and asked, 'Val?'

'It resonates, Lynda saying this.'

'You need an officer with experience,' Lynda continued, polite but firm. 'Somebody to keep the complaints to a minimum. Maintain everyone's focus on the target.'

'Good luck with that,' Sandra offered.

'I've handled worse,' Lynda said. 'Somalia, two tours. Ecuador, eighteen months. A lot worse.'

'Lady does have a way with a point,' Sandra said.

'So now we're twelve,' Chakkan said. He looked at the two young men. 'You best go make sure you understand what Elizabeth is doing, since you're taking her place.'

'We handled all but two of the fertilizer shipments,' Singh pointed out.

'That was then and this is now,' Chakkan replied.

Durrant said, 'Dr Larkin doesn't like us.'

'Beth doesn't like anybody.' For once the Thai engineer was not smiling. 'Go make sure you understand what needs to happen so you can bring us home.'

Even with everyone's help, it was approaching full daybreak before all their gear was carted into the house. Val would have never expected the thatched hut could have held half what they carried inside. As soon as the last load was dumped, Val said, 'We're off to repair our broken night's sleep.'

'Sure you don't want to join us lotus eaters?' Chakkan waved at the sweeping central staircase. 'There are enough bedrooms for twice our number. Monogrammed silk sheets. Gold-plated faucets. Be it ever so humble.'

'Thanks, but we've kind of settled. When do you want us back?'

'We should be ready to leave around . . .' Chakkan checked his phone, frowned in concentration, decided, 'Seven this evening. Right, Sandra?'

'Sounds good.' Sandra fell into step beside Val, while Elizabeth's strident complaints accompanied them to the front foyer. 'I'll definitely be ready to bid that woman a not-fond farewell by then.'

As she and Lynda started back toward the gates, Val found herself shifting away, drawn by what she decided to call a harmonic resonance. A message that formed around impressions, and only afterwards was mentally compacted into words.

Lynda said, 'Earth to Val.'

She did her best to refocus. 'Sorry, what?'

Lynda smiled as she unlocked their vehicle. 'Something happened, didn't it?'

'Yes.' Val reached for her phone. 'I need to make a call.'

THIRTY-TWO

'We were eight klicks out. Less. Walking to either side of what served as a road. The forest was too dense to spread my team any further. Not and hold to schedule.'

As Barry gave them mission debrief, Darren played drone footage of that same timeframe. All of Kelly's team were seated in their version of a war room. A few of Rabbit's team stood by the rear wall. The front screens were split into segments. The left side held Avri Rowe, Agnes Pendalon, General Skarren, all sharing the same grim intent. The remaining wall-sized image tracked agents making steady progress, holding to either side of a narrow forest trail. A digital clock ran along the top right boundary, showing three thirty in the morning. Barry's team were bright heat images against a dark world.

Barry said, 'We came around a tight jink in the road, and the trail entered a broad clearing. I sent Garten and Stinson on a quick reconnoiter.'

The screen showed nine bodies closing in together as two swept out in opposite directions. The duo held to the forest perimeter, then came back straight through the clearing.

Kelly asked, 'Scouts didn't see anything?'

'Nothing,' Pamela Garten replied.

'Everything was five by five,' Stinson agreed.

'Spooky quiet,' Pamela said.

Kelly thought they all looked shattered. Barry did a better job of keeping his game face intact. Just the same, their total mission failure and days spent in solitary confinement inside a Canadian military prison had shaken them to their core.

Barry said, 'So we started across.' The group elongated, putting two paces between each agent. They entered the clearing, and . . .

Darren said, 'Right here is where we lost contact.' Three

seconds passed, then the main portion of the front screens went dark.

Barry said, 'We didn't just lose contact with HQ. Our night vision gear went blank.'

Stinson said, 'Ditto for our rifle scopes. Heat, laser, the works.'

'And our body mikes,' Pamela said. 'Only contact was by raising our voices.'

'Which meant we had to close ranks again,' Barry said. 'Probably what they intended.'

Skarren muttered, 'How can they do that?'

'We're working on it,' Agnes said. 'Continue.'

'We moved in tight, like I said. We were halfway across the field when they hit us from all sides.'

Stinson said, 'Choppers lit us up like Christmas ornaments.'

Barry said, 'Then the tanks rolled in. Twenty, thirty, too many to count.'

'They pushed through the underbrush,' Pamela said. 'Totally encircling us.'

'Troops with weapons at the ready followed them in,' Stinson said. 'Formed a tight circle around us.'

'Up to the point when the choppers showed up overhead, we hadn't heard a thing,' Barry said. 'One minute the forest was totally silent. The next, there was the thunder of tanks and choppers and troops shouting through multiple megaphones.'

General Skarren said, 'Overwhelming show of force. They wanted your surrender without firing a shot.'

'Yeah, well, it worked,' Barry said.

Agnes said, 'I've personally examined the satellite imagery. It shows no indication of armored troop movement. One moment, you're the only dots on the landscape. The next, boom. There they all are.'

Avri said, 'They've managed to hide an entire settlement. We should have anticipated they could do the same with an attacking force.'

'They didn't attack,' Skarren corrected. 'They arrested.'

Agnes demanded, 'What happened next?'

'They loaded us into troop carriers and drove forever. Two stops, we were brought out one at a time for breaks. Gave us water bottles and MREs. Didn't speak except to say get out, load up, eat. Toward sunset, we pulled into a military compound. I still don't know where exactly it was located. We were photographed, fingerprinted, strip searched, and fitted with the same yellow POW coveralls we were wearing when you picked us up at Dulles. End of story.'

'What is your assessment of the ops?' When Barry remained silent, Agnes pressed, 'You've had enough time to think about it. Let's hear your take—'

'They set a trap, and we walked right into it,' Barry said. 'Total mission failure.'

'We gave you the best intel we had.' Darren's protest carried no heat. 'Always have, always will.'

'We're not blaming anyone,' Agnes said. 'Go on, Barry.'

'When we made that clean slip across the border, we assumed we were in the clear. I think they knew from the start. They let us in, they tracked us north, waited while we geared up. Caught us red-handed, weapons hot, on final approach to the target.'

'No way we could deny your objective,' Skarren said.

'A near-perfect takedown,' Darren agreed.

Skarren said, 'They wanted hostages.'

'There you go,' Barry agreed.

Avri said, 'Then why let you go?'

When the group stayed silent, Kelly offered, 'It was time to send us the next message. We've known they've chosen sides. Now they're saying this could have been a lot worse. And telling us in the clearest way possible. They're ready. For whatever comes next.'

THIRTY-THREE

Kelly endured another twenty minutes of Skarren and Agnes and Avri Rowe engaging in endless circular argument. The chamber was filled with so many jagged emotions Kelly was glad to slip away. As far as she was concerned, their incessant wrangling confirmed one thing they were unwilling to accept.

They were no longer in control.

Kelly definitely shared their frustration, fear, rage, all of that and more. What made her status different were the additional questions for which she had no ready answer.

She covered the eight blocks to Vivienne's office in less than twenty minutes. Today's wind carried a distinct northerly bite, a foretaste of changing seasons. Traffic was heavy, the sidewalks filled with people working their phones, caught in tight bubbles of their own making. Just like her.

She entered the therapist's outer office, seated herself, and listened to the low murmur of voices coming through the wall behind her head. The soft drone carried a calming reassurance. She was sheltered here. For this one brief instant, she could let her mind roam. In safety.

Kelly closed her eyes and relived what she now considered to be the first warning sign. The moment when she came face to face with the realization that control of the situation could well slip from their grasp. That all the government's might, their unified stance with so many other nations and their intelligence agencies, did not represent the only way forward.

Just over a year back, nine minutes past six in the morning, Kelly had entered a LA security company's headquarters. She had intended to confront and possibly arrest the attorney Connor Breach. Instead, Connor had effectively blindsided her. Connor had been accompanied by her own private security detail and an LA detective. She had met Kelly with a righteous fury and matched Kelly's verbal assault blow for blow. Possibly bettering Kelly in the process.

Kelly relived what she had seen in Connor's gaze and attitude. Heard in her voice. Connor Breach did not care about Kelly's federal task force, backed up by the FBI and the White House. *Connor did not care*. Why? Because the woman was convinced that she was right. Her cause or whatever Kelly wanted to call it . . .

The door to her left opened. Kelly lifted her head off the wall as Rabbit emerged. He spotted Kelly and grimaced.

Kelly asked, 'That bad?'

Rabbit left without responding.

Kelly rose and spoke to the empty room. 'Apparently so.'

As usual, Vivienne launched straight in. 'I'd like to start where we left off last time.'

Only today, Kelly responded, 'So would I.'

'Would you? Excellent. Tell me what's on your mind.'

'PPD,' Kelly said. 'How can you tell if this is a real issue for me personally?'

Vivienne rewarded her with a smile. 'You are asking for the criteria that signal a patient experiencing paranoid personality disorder, correct?'

Now that she was here, struggling to unwrap the jumble of conflicting thoughts and emotions, the words did not come easy. 'Yes and no. What I most want to understand is if PPD has colored my decisions.'

A keener light entered the therapist's gaze. 'In other words, how can you look *beyond* any impact PPD might be having on your overall view, correct?'

'Right. Yes.'

Three minutes into their session, Vivienne was right there with her. 'This is very good, Kelly. We are starting on the same page.' Vivienne reached for her pad and pen, made a quick note, then, 'Sorry for repeating myself. But just so we are absolutely clear on a key point; there is no certainty you are actually suffering from PPD.'

'I feel like, maybe . . .'

She nodded approval to Kelly's unfinished thought. 'The most important issue by far is that you are open to the possibility.'

'But how do I know?'

'In other words, what concerns you most in this immediate moment is how can you know if past traumatic experiences and their resulting influence on previous professional directives are impacting your vision of current events. Correct?'

Kelly nodded. Yes.

'You are here because you feel you owe this to your team. This loyalty to your group, this determination to endure what must be a series of difficult therapy sessions on their behalf as well as your own, is one of the traits that I admire most about you. You seek to lead them safely by maintaining a clear sense of vision and purpose. It is what holds you here, despite everything you encounter inside this room. Your sense of loyalty and duty are admirable.'

'You've never said that before.'

'Perhaps that is a failing of my profession. The need to maintain strict objectivity makes it hard to offer compliments.' Vivienne made another note. 'Back to the issue at hand. In today's session, I suggest we forgo any discussion of theory or general criteria regarding PPD.'

'Specifics,' Kelly agreed.

'Which means we must examine the possibility of tainted perspective, or emotionally clouded judgment, by way of an issue directly related to your current state.'

'Who is the enemy,' Kelly replied. Walking with her. Moving forward. Taking aim. Despite the racing heart, the tremors.

'What if you could resume your telepathic bond?' Vivienne set her pad aside. 'What if you were granted the opportunity to rejoin? And all you had to do in order to make this happen was to accept that they are not, in fact, the enemy?'

The sudden craving was so intense that Kelly felt an instantaneous need to deflect. 'The trees . . . They're gone.'

'For the sake of today's session, let's say that is not the case. Say the smallest fragment of all the remaining leaves, or whatever you want to call them, is enough. You are granted a single fleck of dust from the tree, you acknowledge this group is not a foe, you ingest it, and your telepathic abilities resume in full. How does that make you feel?'

'Is this for real, or some hypothetical you just dreamed up?'

'Please don't deflect, Kelly.' A moment's hesitation, then, 'All right. In this case, perhaps I should respond. Since you informed me about the arrest of your team, I have searched for developments within the Canadian medical system. I wanted to see if the authorities were directly involved.'

The medical avenue was something she suspected Darren had overlooked. 'And?'

'There is very little. And what I've managed to find appears to be unsubstantiated rumor. But there are suggestions or hints that a tiny fragment of a leaf is enough to induce this telepathic bonding.'

She felt her world severely shaken. Whether in a good or bad way, she could not say.

Vivienne showed her an open palm. 'Again, these are rumors only. Right now, let's please focus on the core issue, the point that brought you in here today. Say this is so. Say the opportunity is out there.'

Kelly felt that all too familiar struggle to remain open, listen, even breathe. She planted a fist at the base of her ribcage. Trying desperately to stifle the burn.

The *draw*.

'Back to my purely hypothetical question. Just for this moment, imagine that it is reality. Someone approaches you. Offers you this chance. All you have to do—'

'Stop. Please. Just . . . stop.'

Vivienne held to her silent observation for a very long minute. Then, 'You ingested the leaf or whatever it was in pursuit of those you *assumed* were indirect accomplices to your fiancé's murder. Then your actions against this group stripped away your newfound ability.' A pause, then, 'Do you see where this is headed?'

Kelly tried to focus. She really did. 'I . . . No.'

'A gun in the hands of a cold-blooded killer, a drug lord and human trafficker, results in one outcome. That same weapon in the hands of a duty-bound officer of the law means something else entirely.' Vivienne leaned forward, close enough to tap Kelly's wrist in time to her words. 'So long as right motives lead to right actions.'

THIRTY-FOUR

Ten thirty that morning, Carlton was riding in a well-equipped bus on the approach to Richmond. Directly behind the driver was a sitting area with six leather captain's chairs positioned around an expandable table. Behind that was a kitchen, a full bathroom, office, even a bunkroom. The bus with driver had a daily rental rate of eight and a half thousand dollars. The two-day swing through Virginia, North and South Carolina was intended as a test run. It granted them a much-needed chance to work on Dale's public face before they hit full-on campaign speed. Terrance Dale was only scheduled to make three appearances each day. The press seated with Dale up front had been carefully vetted.

Carlton was back in the office, giving Terrance's first stump speech a final polish, when Val called. She asked, 'How is it going?'

'Ask me after our first stop in Richmond,' Carlton replied. 'You know what they say, no war-room strategy remains intact once the bullets start flying.'

'Two words I'm not comfortable with,' Val replied. 'War and bullets.'

'Terrance is playing host to five journalists,' Carlton went on. 'All they really want to talk about is . . . you know.'

'Grenada,' Val said. 'Yes. I know.'

'Terrance is a pro. He sticks to his script, talks about innovation and free enterprise. They want more, of course. Speaking of which—'

'Carlton. Don't.'

He said it anyway. 'Do you really have to go?'

'Yes. I must.' Firm and done. 'Changing the subject, I wanted to give you a heads-up. I'm about to call CBS.'

He leaned over and slid the door shut. 'Are you asking or telling?'

'Carlton, don't object. Or argue with me. Please.'

'You're certain this is the right move, then.'

'More than certain. It's part of the . . .'

'Pressure. Flow. Whatever.' He sighed. 'I was hoping we'd have more time to get our campaign on a stable footing.'

'Sorry, no.'

'Can I ask why? A lot is riding on this.'

'Remember, we leave late tomorrow.'

Carlton needed a long moment to fit air back in his chest, enough to say, 'So soon.'

'Yes. And the impression that I must do this before departure was a crucial part of the message. Pressure. Flow. Whatever.'

Despite everything, hearing Val repeat his words caused him to smile. 'In that case, you'll need to excuse me. I had best go prep my candidate for the firestorm that's about to erupt.'

'Please tell Terrance to win this thing,' Val said. 'For all good people everywhere.'

Val waited until she had returned to the hotel for a shower and a meal and a rest. While Lynda met with Connor and Denton for a debrief, Val called CBS.

The receptionist was a young male with a flat Valley accent. Crisp and impatient. Biding time at the front desk until his agent called.

Val gave her name, then asked, 'Could I speak with a producer in your news department?'

'What is this in regard to?'

'I assume you've watched your network's coverage of the six silos being turned into a spaceship. I was the person interviewed in Iowa.'

A long silence, then, 'Hold, please.'

Val carried the phone into the suite's bedroom and spent the next few minutes going through her newly acquired wardrobe. Her journey down Rodeo Drive had resulted in two full outfits with several add-ons. At the time, it had all seemed absurd. She was, after all, departing for Saturn. Plus the second outfit was unlike anything she had ever owned, a semi-formal Ferragamo of navy silk and linen blend with silver highlights to both the slacks and jacket. Cloth buttons of silver weave climbed all the way to a standing silver collar. On the rack it had looked mildly outlandish. But when she tried it on, Lynda had applauded, and the salesman pretended to swoon.

A woman came on then. Sharp and incisive as an ice blade. 'Ms Garnier?'

'Yes.'

'How do I know this is you?'

'I'm going to send you a thirty-minute video that you need to watch. It will confirm my identity and a great deal more.'

A pause, then, 'It certainly sounds like the woman who rocked our world. From Iowa, of all places. You do realize all the networks have been scouring the planet in search of you.'

'If you're willing,' Val said, 'I could swing by, and you can check me out in person.'

'You're actually in LA?'

'For a very brief period only.'

'You're willing to bounce in for an interview. Just like that.'

'Your lucky day,' Val said.

'Santa won't need to stop by my house this Christmas,' the woman agreed. 'Do you have a pen?'

After she wrote down the woman's email address, Val said, 'I can only give you an hour.'

'You're making the rounds, I take it.'

'No, this is an exclusive. My time is beyond tight. We depart LA this evening, and leave for Saturn tomorrow.'

A pause, then, 'Send me the feed. Get here as soon as you can. We'll be ready.'

The CBS Television City studio complex was located at 7800 Beverly Boulevard, at the corner of North Fairfax. Val felt her first twinge of fear when the stern black-and-white structure fronting the street came into view.

Lynda must have noticed her nerves, for she said, 'You've totally got this cold.'

An angular woman with close-cropped auburn hair paced the front lobby as they pulled into the lot. She came outside and inspected Val on approach. 'So it's really you.'

'Val Garnier. This is Lynda Eliott.'

'Frida Blanche. We can't cover what we need in just one hour.'

'That's all I can give you. Sorry.'

Frida's narrow features pinched tight in irritation. But all she said was, 'Let's move inside.'

Frida handed them visitor passes and led them past the security checkpoint, through the glass barrier, and down a central corridor. 'Delay the launch. Those aliens can wait another day. I bet they don't even have clocks.'

'Was that a joke?'

Frida was dressed in a rough silk outfit of autumn colors and moved one step off a full run. She ignored the multitude of faces that peered from every doorway. 'I'm too frantic for humor.'

A young woman thundered towards them, clutching a phone in one hand and a sheaf of papers in the other. Her hair was a mess, her eyes panicky. 'The studio's prepped!'

'Reynolds?'

'Totally freaking out!'

'Why should I be the only one?'

'We're talking full-on heart attack!' The young woman fell into step beside Frida. 'And a seizure!'

'Tell him to save me one of each.' Frida pushed open a door, said, 'In here.'

The overly bright room contained two middle-aged women standing wide-eyed and ready in front of an illuminated wall-sized mirror. Frida said, 'Hair and makeup.' To the women, 'You have five minutes.'

One wailed, 'You said ten!'

'That was then, this is now. Five and counting.'

Val hurriedly dressed in her new duds and allowed the women to fluff, comb, paint, prep. Three minutes in, a man and a face she had watched for years entered and asked, 'Is this really an exclusive?'

'I don't have time for anything else. I'm Val Garnier. This is Lynda Eliott.'

'Reynolds Hatch.' He was a slender, silver-haired calm at the eye of the studio hurricane. 'In case I forget to mention later, thanks for giving me the scoop of a lifetime.'

'I'm so glad it's you,' Val said.

'Really?' He leaned against the side wall and crossed his arms. 'Why is that?'

'You always seem to know what you're talking about.'

'Not today.'

'Your interest in your guest, the respect you show even when you're applying the scalpel, always seems genuine.'

'No knives today,' he said. 'I'm too awestruck.'

Frida yelled from the hallway, 'I'm waiting!'

The studio was set up in standard interview format – two comfy armchairs were stationed just far enough apart for their knees not to touch. As Val was miked and the lights adjusted, she asked, 'Can I make one suggestion for a final point?'

Frida stood just outside the light's perimeter. 'Listening.'

A man called from the shadows, 'Sound is good.'

Val said, 'I'm going with them. To Enceladus.'

That little news item froze the entire studio. Then Frida snapped, 'All of you can faint on your own time.'

Reynolds told his producer, 'I just forgot every question we discussed. Poof. Gone.'

Frida said, 'Tough.' Her hand reached across the shadows, pointing to the wild-haired young woman. 'Count them in.'

THIRTY-FIVE

The interview ran pretty much as Val might have expected, if she'd had time to anticipate or prep. Reynolds' questions were gently spoken and deeply probing. Val listened carefully and tried to respond honestly. She knew some of her answers were too long, but she didn't try to edit herself. She left that to the pros.

The only times Val was not fully open were when Reynolds asked about their opponents. He called them that twice. Then Reynolds switched for a third question, calling them attackers. Each time Val was polite but firm. She refused to even suggest who might have been behind destroying the desert rowan or shooting a plane out of the sky. Or discuss their motives.

In the end, Reynolds politely gave up. When Frida asked for another try, Reynolds shook his head, then ignored her. Frida hissed. When Frida then waved her arms over her head, Reynolds and Val shared a tiny smile.

He said, 'Talk us through what this experience is like. How does it feel to link telepathically?' Then, 'You've talked a great deal about what it isn't. How you can't read another person's thoughts. What *can* you do?'

Then, 'You've used that term, *the draw*, several times. Can you give us a better idea of what you mean?'

Then, 'This eleven-month silence must have been difficult. Describe that for us.'

Then, 'How can you be certain you are now communicating with an alien race on one of Saturn's moons?'

Then, 'How can you trust them?'

Like that.

Finally, the producer spoke from the shadows. 'Five minutes.'

Reynolds smoothly switched to Val's suggestion for a final topic. 'You're going on this interplanetary voyage.'

'We leave sunset tomorrow,' she confirmed.

'A billion miles,' he said.

'Each way,' she agreed.

'How long will you be gone?'

Val knew because she'd heard Chakkan and Sandra discussing it. 'Five days out, four back. Our time on Enceladus is uncertain. We won't know until we begin drilling through the ice.'

'You're traveling from Earth to Saturn in five days?'

'About. Yes. Once clear of Earth's atmosphere, we'll accelerate to about twenty-five Gs. Remember what you saw in the video. Our craft's internal state is completely free of any external force. Or radiation. The protective globe can be altered somewhat, allowing in the frequencies of visual light. But that also reduces our protective shielding. So for most of the trip we will be flying blind. Then, once we arrive, we've factored in a full day for a pinpoint landing.'

'According to what the . . .'

'We're calling them Enceladons.'

'So what these aliens tell you . . .'

'Telepathically. Without words. Right.'

'How do you know what or how much they need?'

That was easy enough. 'People smarter than me have worked out the ingredients by way of atomic structures. Figuring the amounts required was handled pretty much the same way. They started with the molecular mass of water.'

A pause then, 'You'll be making this voyage in a craft that can only be described as makeshift.'

'Right.'

'You have to admit there is a very real chance you and your team . . . How many are you?'

'Twelve.' She had said it before, but did not mind the repetition. 'Four on transport, four on ice mining and delivery. One hyper-sensitive young man who has maintained the clearest sense of contact with the Enceladons. A professor of maths serving as admin and cook. A security expert to keep us all as grounded as possible. And me. Official observer.'

'Who is your captain?'

Val liked having a reason to smile. 'That is an excellent question. I'll have to get back to you on that.'

Her response made him more somber still. 'There's a real chance none of you will make it back home.' He gave her an instant to reply. When Val remained silent, he pressed, 'This journey carries enormous risk. Three final questions, Val. First, why go? And second, what if you don't return?'

Val liked how he linked the two questions because, 'The answer is the same for both. I've experienced a growing sense of before and after. One form of human existence, at least for me and my crew, is ending. This has to happen. Maybe in time I'll work out everything those words mean. Right now, it's enough to say that I recognize this is happening. It is the only way this new life can take hold and grow.

'Am I scared? Yes. I am absolutely terrified.' She paused for a very hard breath. Then, 'But this journey is not just about doing our best to save an alien race who share our planetary system. This is also about all of us, the human race, and who we are becoming. Our journey forms a vital component of how our tomorrow will be shaped.'

Val had the sense of the entire studio taking a long breath. Caught in the motionless amber of a moment beyond time. Then Frida said, 'Time to wrap this up.'

Val felt as if she could see the third and final question there in Reynolds' gaze. Taste it in the studio's air. When he remained silent, she said gently, 'It's OK.'

He did not respond.

'Go ahead,' she said. 'Ask.'

He almost whispered, 'Can I do this?'

The studio rang with a myriad of gasps.

Val replied, 'You can. Yes.'

'But the trees are gone.'

'All the remaining leaves have been fragmented. One speck of rowan dust is all it takes.' She reached into her pocket, withdrew the tiny plastic sleeve. 'Ready?'

Reynolds leaned forward. 'I feel like I've been waiting for this my entire life.'

THIRTY-SIX

Kelly watched the hour-long CBS special with all but seven of her team. Some of Barry's and Rabbit's crews were out on leave and did not make it back in time. As soon as Kelly received the alert, she had instructed Darren to make sure everyone, including the White House, was aware.

Throughout the entire special, their ops center remained silent, motionless. Agnes, Skarren and Avri Rowe occupied the same three left-hand screens as the previous day. The program ended with an announcement that CBS would air live coverage of the Grenada space launch from three o'clock East Coast time the next afternoon, beginning with a repeat of today's special and the video supplied by Val Garnier.

When the station switched to commercials, as soon as Darren muted the screens, Agnes Pendalon declared, 'This changes everything.'

The two men positioned above and below Agnes' image remained grimly silent.

Agnes went on, 'The other networks are going to be out for blood. They'll want something, anything that eats away at CBS's monopoly.'

Skarren nodded. 'The Canada ops is bound to emerge. All it takes is one soldier or some low-level Ottawa bureaucrat to start blabbing.'

Kelly watched as Avri was handed a paper. He read and scowled. Shook his head. He told them, 'Hold that thought.'

As Kelly watched the president's chief of staff mute his screen, her mind tracked back to the program's final image. Reynolds Hatch, *Sixty Minutes* news anchor, a name and face familiar to millions, accepted the small plastic packet from Val Garnier. As he followed the woman's instructions, the camera zoomed in tight on the shimmering strand his hands now cupped. She and everyone else held their breath as he lifted the strand

and breathed it in. The memory was enough to brand Kelly's entire body with . . .

The draw.

The therapist's words pounded her brain. Given another chance, would she?

Even more powerful was Vivienne's underlying question. Could she accept this global group, who now held the power to grow their numbers exponentially, was not in fact the enemy? That Agnes and Skarren, and, yes! Even her! Kelly Kaiser! They all had it wrong? They had spent over a year hunting people who were not in fact . . .

Avri Rowe broke into Kelly's thoughts with, 'Congresswoman Bowers. Remember her?'

For the sake of Rabbit's newcomers, Kelly offered, 'Bowers and her family traveled to the Kurils soon after the first rowan appeared.'

Avri continued, 'Bowers just notified the White House that tomorrow she is asking Congress to open an official hearing . . .' He lifted the page and read, 'Covering any and all operations leading to destruction of the rowan trees. She intends to subpoena testimony from several members of the president's cabinet.'

The ops room was still digesting this when Avri's attention was again drawn away. He turned back to the camera and said, 'I'm called to the Oval Office.' The screen went blank.

A silent moment later, Barry announced, 'All the major networks just sent out an alert. The vice president is about to do a live interview.'

THIRTY-SEVEN

Carlton made it a point to be settled in the Raleigh Hilton before Val's CBS interview was aired at seven thirty that evening. The vice president's suite was large enough for him to invite the local journalists and TV newscasters and their camera crews to join them. Carlton thought their guests' response offered the day's first hint of humor. Everyone except CBS shared the identical expression: a mix of astonishment and bitterness over someone else gaining the scoop. The CBS crew made no attempt to hide their smug joy.

Val's interview was preceded by an airing of their video. Carlton was pleased with how professional it appeared, and enjoyed watching as it pounded the reporters and journalists with news they had failed to obtain on their own.

As soon as the interview ended, they asked Terrance for a response. Live and on air. Dale agreed without hesitation.

The gathered press needed a little over half an hour to set up and coordinate feeds with their national networks. Terrance returned to the bedroom. Carlton remained where he was, supervising and texting and fielding calls. Doing what little he could to prepare his team for the coming firestorm.

Terrance Dale held to the same theme as before, expressing his surprise and delight at the huge progress in technical know-how this represented. But Terrance refused to be drawn on Val's claim of a secret response team actively seeking to thwart this new movement. He stated repeatedly that he had never been party to any such action, and could not discuss something he had never been involved with. The interviewers grew tired of his stonewalling and returned to the night's main question. Did he believe this was real?

Terrance hesitated for the first time since the barrage of questions had started. Stern, calm, the stalwart leader who had remained silent in the face of everything he had endured. Four long years.

Dale was dressed in a fresh shirt but the same navy suit he had worn all day. He stroked the striped tie, running his hand down from neck to navel. Twice. A third time. Then, 'We have witnessed the impossible. A new form of energy and transport linked in a way we have never before fathomed. Globes appearing from a source we have yet to identify. Lifting six silos and their entire foundations with no observable damage to the surrounding structures. Landing them intact on an uninhabited Caribbean island. Filling them with twelve thousand tons of fertilizer brought from all over the globe. Do I think they are taking these nutrients to Saturn's moon? My answer to this is unequivocal. Yes. I do think they are going to try.'

Another pause, a distinct and somber punctuation. 'Do I think there are opponents to this new form of transport and whatever it represents? I have no idea. But if you accept Ms Garnier's claims as true, that this is derived from a visitation by other beings, then yes. There is a distinct possibility that certain governments view this as a threat to their power structure.'

One of the male television anchors broke in, 'But Mr Vice President—'

Carlton spoke for the first time since the live interview began. 'Let him finish or this interview is terminated.'

The journalist flushed beet-red over being scolded on air. But he did not speak again.

Terrance continued, 'The global order is founded upon a balance of weapons and military might. What we are witnessing upends this equilibrium. Some governments' knee-jerk reaction will be to consider this a threat. People who have taken the same step as Mr Reynolds Hatch will be classed as a new enemy. But they have done nothing that I can see to justify such an attitude. Viewing them as foes represents the fatal flaw within many current regimes. Treating change as a threat. Seeing any potential opponent as a new enemy. That is wrong thinking. It reveals a weakness at the core of our political systems. I condemn it in the strongest possible terms.'

Terrance Dale pointed to the blank screen. 'I ask any and all of you to show me one iota of evidence that these people represent a threat to our nation, our civilization, our human race.

Everything I have seen suggests they act out of the highest of motives, what defines the finest elements of us as a people. They serve those in need. They show compassion. They seek only to assist.'

Carlton rose to his feet. 'Thank you, ladies and gentlemen. This interview is now concluded.'

THIRTY-EIGHT

Lynda called Chakkan as soon as they left the CBS building. She listened for a long moment, thanked him, and cut the connection. 'Our flight time to Grenada has been pushed back.'

'Flight time,' Val repeated. 'Nice.'

'Something to do with calibrating bubbles so we all travel in the same general direction,' Lynda went on. 'Of course, I might have gotten that totally wrong. Chakkan also said something about hamsters and their little wheels.'

'When are we due back?'

'He only said it would be hours yet.' Lynda pulled into traffic. 'And it shouldn't change our lift-off. Which is still set for tomorrow. Hungry?'

'Very. Almost as much as I am tired.'

'In that case, I have just the thing.'

Lynda returned to their Beverly Hills hotel and checked them back into Val's former suite. Val took a long shower, slipped into a fluffy hotel robe, and stretched out on the bed. She wasn't sleepy so much as boneless.

She drifted, content to stay there as long as time allowed. Which was when she was struck by yet another incoming force. The same as before, only different. A simple addition to everything that had come before, not so much a requirement as a soft little nudge.

Val was on her feet when Lynda entered and said, 'They just aired your whole shebang a second time, video and all.' She pointed at the muted screen. 'They're about to rerun the vice president's response.'

They were seated and watching Terrance do an excellent job of fielding impossible questions when the room-service waiter arrived with their meal. Val ate a little, enough to stifle the strongest pangs, but as soon as Carlton concluded the interview, Val said, 'I need to do something.'

Lynda merely smiled. 'Do tell.'

'You feel it?'

'Girl, we'll have some long days ahead to discuss feelings. Go do whatever it is that's got the room's energy fizzing.'

THIRTY-NINE

'Chakkan, it's Val.'

'Don't ask me for a specific LA departure time. You can't. I'll shout at you. I hate shouting.'

'That's not why I'm calling.'

'Oh. OK. Go ahead then.'

'I think . . . No. I know. Or, I sense. Something.'

Chakkan brightened measurably. 'Now you sound like me. I sense we need to get this calibration right before we bounce into the night sky. On account of how I like making Elizabeth wrong. Almost as much as I like breathing.'

They had the call on speaker, which granted Lynda the chance to reply, 'Breathing is good. Nix on the risk of not breathing.'

Val said, 'We need to alert the press to our departure from LA. Keep the public abreast of what we're doing.'

A long pause, then, 'I don't even want to know. Is that clear enough, or do you need a diagram?'

'I guess not telling you anything more works for me.'

'Now excuse me while I go see if I can improve on my yelling abilities.'

'Chakkan, wait. I need an estimate . . .'

Lynda asked, 'Did he just hang up on us?'

Val made basically the same call to each of the networks. She introduced herself, waited through the mechanical music interludes, introduced herself again, then started in with her alert.

Speaking with CBS was a pleasure. The others treated her as barely above a nuisance, calling after everyone had gone home. She was about to make her final call to the *LA Times* when Chakkan rang on Lynda's phone and said it was time for them to scurry back, because the train was leaving the station. For better or worse. His exact words.

She followed Lynda from the room. 'Thanks for such a semi-magical interlude. It was exactly what the doctor ordered.'

Lynda gave her smug. 'And you thought the girl was only good for banging heads.'

'I know what Chakkan would say to that.' Val entered the elevator and did her best to mimic the Thai engineer. 'No banging. Head banging is verboten.'

While Lynda checked them out, Val placed the night's final call.

'Newsroom.'

'This is Val Garnier. I'd like to speak—'

'Stop right there. For the fourth time tonight, I need confirmation you are who you say you are.'

'Call the Maybourne Hotel on Canon. Tell the operator to switch you to the front desk. Ask for me.' She cut the connection and informed Lynda, 'This gets old.'

'Never mind, dear.' Lynda pocketed her credit card. 'It will all be over soon.'

Thirty seconds later, the hotel receptionist answered her phone, listened, asked, 'Ms Garnier?'

'That's me.' Val accepted the phone and asked the voice on the other end, 'Are we good?'

A different voice, female and ageless and smoke-roughened, demanded, 'Why weren't we given the exclusive, is what my editor wants to know.'

'I'm calling with the next best thing,' Val replied. 'We're about to launch three more – what should I call them?'

'You're asking me? That's rich.'

'OK, bubbles. I'm calling to invite you to witness their take-offs.'

Now she was excited. 'You're talking here in LA?'

'Actually, it's three events and six bubbles.' Val read off the Bel Air address. 'Gather outside the gates. I'm on my way there now. If there's time, I'll stop and answer questions before we depart.'

'Wait! How—'

Everyone in the lobby watched Val cut the connection and thank the hovering receptionist for the use of her phone. Lynda asked, 'Can we go now?'

FORTY

A train of cars and news vans blocked both sides of the Bel Air street. Lynda parked well clear of the crowd by the estate's closed front gates. Reynolds Hatch was seated on the rear platform of his news van, keeping well clear of the others. He smiled at her approach. 'Well, if it isn't the lady who shook my world. Care for a coffee?'

'I wouldn't say no.'

'Make that two.' Lynda stepped up beside her. 'I sure hope somebody remembered to pack enough brew for the trip. Two billion miles and no coffee might render me unfit for polite company.'

Val waited for the cameraman to fill two plastic mugs, then asked Reynolds, 'How are you faring?'

'That's a hard question to answer.' He pulled out his phone, activated the record app, and set it on a light-box beside him. 'On one level, nothing has changed. On another, everything is different. Amped up a notch. But only if I'm willing to . . .' He searched.

Val offered, 'Open your internal portal. Accept the company of unseen new friends.'

'Exactly.' He took his time for a thoughtful sip. 'And something else. There is an undercurrent of power just out of sight. Every time I mentally look in that direction, I sense this flow of energy moving at incredible speed.'

'You have just summarized what is currently dominating our existence.' Which was when the idea struck. 'Would you like to travel with us to Grenada?'

Reynolds arranged for one of the CBS crew to return their Hertz rental. Then he and Val approached the gathering with Lynda and a cameraman in tow. Inside the gates, two large delivery-type vans were parked to the right of the home's main entry. Connor and the physics postdoc Charles Durrant unloaded bags and parcels from the vehicles, while Denton supervised a conga line shifting the gear inside.

She stopped where the shadows still hid them and said, 'I've got an idea.'

'Oh, good,' Reynolds said. 'My mind hasn't had a single clear thought since you invited me along for the ride.'

Val pointed to the vans and explained what she wanted, then asked Lynda, 'Think that will work?'

'Making a bunch of journalists do what I tell them will be like herding cats. But I'll try.' She looked at Reynolds and his cameraman. 'Present company excepted.'

The cameraman responded with, 'Meow.'

Val asked Reynolds, 'You're clear on what needs to happen?'

'Follow your lead, be ready to bolt.' He grinned. 'As excited and terrified as I feel right now, I'll make it to the front door in no time flat.'

'Ten bucks says I beat you both,' Lynda said.

Val asked, 'What about closing the gates?'

'Have whoever is driving the second van stay in place until you two are by the front door,' Lynda replied. 'Tell Chakkan to code them shut. I'll tell the drivers to take off while I hold the cats in place. Soon as the gates are closed and the kitties all outside, I'll scurry home. Simple.'

Val thought it was anything but. Just the same, Lynda's calm resolve helped steady her on a number of levels. 'Here we go.'

Val stepped forward, introduced herself, smiled in silence at the sudden rush of attention and demands, then allowed the camera operators to position her so the gates and house were behind her. The eastern sky was painted with the first wash of a new dawn as she began, 'We only have a few minutes. I suggest you let me explain why we're here.' She pointed through the gates and said, 'Yesterday we acquired this house and two others. The reason for these choices is, they all contain apartment-size safe rooms built by the same company and more or less to the same specifications. These sanctuaries, as they're commonly known, will be stacked to form our residence for the journey—'

That was as far as they let her go.

Val tried to field a couple of the shouted questions, then Reynolds called,

'Somebody is trying to get your attention.'

Cameras and lights swiveled toward the portico, where Chakkan stood waving one arm while the other shielded his eyes against the television lights. Denton and Connor climbed into the vans and started their motors.

Val said, 'I have to leave. Give me thirty seconds of silence, please; I'll tell you what you're about to see.' Then, 'Each house is going to be split into two sections. The main portion will be taken to a Canadian preserve where some of our team now live. It will be restructured as a multi-family residence or meeting place, something. The sanctuaries will head off to the Caribbean.' As the gates began opening and the vans forward, she finished, 'Now I need you all to step back.'

She ignored the protests, the shouted questions, the strident demands for more information. Lynda positioned herself to block anyone from entering the grounds. Val used the clamor to step in tight to the left-hand gate, positioning the first van between her and the crowd. She was pleased to find Reynolds already there. 'Keep as low as you possibly can.'

Reynolds took a firm grip on the nylon satchel slung from his shoulder and nodded.

As the first van passed through the gates, Val leaned through the open window and told Denton, 'Lynda is desperate to hear somebody brought coffee.'

'Enough for an army. All this was Connor's idea. She called Chakkan, who confessed they had not gotten any further than ready meals and inflatable mattresses. We've spent the entire day spending money. Who knew I was born to shop?'

'Do me a favor and only pull up far enough to let Connor halfway through the gates. Then stop and have a word with the press.'

Denton reached across the passenger seat. 'Anything to help my favorite astronaut.'

Val gripped his hand. 'You are a dear, sweet man and Connor is one fortunate lady.'

'Be sure and come home, Val. Please.'

'You bet.' She stepped back. 'Catch you on the flip side.'

Val walked to Connor's truck, shadowed by the crouched news reporter. She leaned through the open window and said, 'You've done good, lady.'

'Send you off to Saturn with polyester sheets and pots of instant noodles? Puh-lease. How are you?'

'Exhausted, happy, excited, scared, stressed. I probably forgot something, but I'm too tired to think of it just now.'

'Well, you certainly look good doing it.' She did the same as Denton, reaching out and taking hold of Val's hand. 'Tell me you're coming back.'

'You bet your bippy.'

'Not like that. Say it strong enough so I'll keep hold of believing you.'

Val ignored the myriad of camera lights that caught her tears. She embraced all of Connor that she could reach. 'See you in two weeks. Maybe less.'

When Val released her, Connor wiped her eyes, offered an unsteady smile, said, 'I suppose that will have to do.'

'Lynda and I need to get inside while Denton and you occupy the press's attention. Stay where you're partly blocking the entrance. Once we're all safely through, I'll wave from the portico. You and Denton are free to take off.'

'Come home to us, Val. Please.'

Neither tears nor more promises would help either of them. Val stepped back to where the van's windowless rear compartment blocked them from view. She checked that Reynolds was dogging her steps, said, 'Let's run.'

FORTY-ONE

Chakkan greeted her with, 'Connor and Denton told me to pass on something about behaving and returning. Who's this?'

'Reynolds Hatch, meet our pilot, navigator, skipper. Dr Chakkan.'

Chakkan waited until Lynda slipped inside, then closed and locked the door. 'Reynolds is here because . . .'

Now that the interview was over, she felt giddy and exhausted both. 'My new friend needs a lift to Grenada.'

'I actually don't know what to say to that. A first.' Chakkan studied the reporter. 'Have I seen you somewhere before?'

'*Sixty Minutes*,' Val said. '*CBS News Roundup*. Lots of places.'

'Click.' Chakkan almost smiled. 'The sound of a very dim lightbulb coming on.'

'He is also one of us,' Val added.

'Since yesterday,' Reynolds confirmed.

'So are several million others. Val . . .'

'Him being here is part of the flow.'

'Ah. You're certain of that, are you?'

'Absolutely.'

'Well, in that case.' Chakkan offered his hand. 'Welcome to bedlam.'

FORTY-TWO

Ten past four that morning, Kelly gave up on sleep. While coffee brewed, she dressed for a run. The weatherperson had predicted a clear night with the season's first freezing temps. She slipped on tights, sweatshirt, and a knit cap. She finished her coffee and belted on her fanny pack holding phone, ID, some cash, and a lightweight Sig Sauer. Since moving into her apartment, these pre-dawn runs had become a favorite. But this was the outskirts of DC, and a lady had to be careful.

She checked out with security and set off. The night sky was so clear that stars defied the streetlights. An occasional car passed with an apologetic whisper. Her feet beat a steady tempo on the sidewalk.

Her mind returned to the same images that had robbed her night of sleep.

She relived tight snippets from the highly professional video where Val Garnier supplied the voiceover, and her interview with Reynolds Hatch. They played on a continuous loop as Kelly ran. Just as they had all night.

Kelly did her best to concentrate on the issues that mattered most to her team. Starting with their task, if any, that would occupy the coming days. Once that cobbled-together spaceship flew away. Going to Saturn. To rescue another intelligent race who shared their planetary system.

Try as she might, Kelly's mind repeatedly turned to the interview's final scene. Watching Reynolds Hatch ingest the shimmering thread.

Kelly wanted to declare the world-renowned newsman a traitor. That he had just demolished his career. Stepped into the forbidden zone. Entered the dark side. Betrayed them all.

And perhaps all that was true.

But raw honesty defined Kelly Kaiser and remained a core component of who she was. Despite everything. It did not allow her to flinch from what she felt every time she replayed that image.

The draw.

As Kelly turned around and started back, an idea began to take hold. At first glance, the concept was so totally off the wall that she did her best to leave it behind.

She finished her stretches, pushed through the outer door and greeted the agent fresh to the morning duty. The idea continued to whisper. Insistent now. Taking hold with invisible hooks that actually hurt her brain.

The elevator doors opened on her floor. She walked the hall. Entered her apartment. Stood in the foyer. Watching the mental fragments coalesce. Solid enough now to make sense.

Kelly waited until she had showered and dressed to call Rabbit. The kitchen clock read eleven minutes past six.

Rabbit answered with, 'Hi, Kelly. What's up?'

'Sorry to call so early.'

'No sweat. Diyani's been asked to help Barry monitor news feeds and online traffic from Central and South America. Agnes wants an update at nine. Diyani's making huevos rancheros and chorizo and her special corn tortillas. Want to join us?'

'Tempting.' Diyani was a superb cook. Since the couple had moved into a fifth-floor apartment, Kelly had been a regular at their table. 'But I need to speak with you about something confidential.'

'Want me to bring you a plate?'

'If she's offering, most definitely.'

'Five minutes.'

Rabbit arrived with two steaming portions. They sat at the counter and ate in companionable silence. The food was excellent, as usual. Kelly waited until they were halfway through to say, 'If it's OK, I'd like to talk with you about Vivienne.'

'Outstanding,' Rabbit said between bites. 'So would I.'

That caught her off guard. 'Really?'

'Absolutely. I was hoping that was why you called.'

She slid off the stool and carried her mug into the kitchen. 'I've spent the past hour worrying over how to tiptoe my way around the confidentiality issue.' She lifted the pot. 'Refill?'

'I'm good, thanks. This is me telling you to forget the ballet.'

She resumed her seat. 'Great.'

'Did Vivienne ask you how you'd feel about, you know . . .'

'Taking another dose of the leaf. As a matter of fact, she did.'

'Any chance she mentioned Canadian medical chatrooms discussing the fragmentation of remaining leaves?'

Kelly set her mug down, the motions slow, overly careful. 'She did. Yes.'

'OK, so last night I decided to check. It's all over the sites now. Mostly either debating whether it's real or asking how they can get their hands on a fragment. But you know what? Before the CBS interview and video went out, there was nothing. Nada.'

'Are you sure?'

'Come on, Kelly. This was my job, remember? I checked. Thoroughly. Not a peep.'

The sudden flood of anger lifted her from the stool. Kelly arched her back, lifted her hands over her head, stretched. Trying to make room for the rage. 'Let's back up for a second. How did you first hear about Vivienne?'

'From Diyani.' The answer came instantly. Telling her Rabbit had been occupied with the same concern she was only now recognizing. 'She volunteers at a local shelter helping with undocumented women and their kids.'

'I didn't know that.'

'Diyani's a quiet one, sure enough. Anyway, there was this Metro patrolman who had become an ally. Someone she could trust with the sensitive cases. A vet, left the Marines after three hard tours. You know how it goes. Late at night, quiet hours, chatting. He told her about coming home with issues that threatened to wreck his life. How this therapist in Pentagon City was making a real difference, probably saving his marriage.'

Kelly began pacing. 'OK, so you make contact. And this highly regarded therapist, totally overbooked, happens to have time for a new patient.'

'Two patients.'

'First you, then on the strength of what you tell her, Vivienne takes on me as well. And not just once a week like normal. Insisting we both come in five times each week.'

Rabbit rose to his feet. 'I should have questioned—'

'Hold that thought.' When she reached the side wall, Kelly pounded it. Quick strikes in time to her words. 'The day that global silence lifted among telepaths. How did your new team members respond when they reconnected?'

'They were bouncing off the walls.'

'I was in with Vivienne, remember?'

Rabbit's eyes could not have grown any larger. 'I came and pulled you out of therapy.'

'That entire session, Vivienne was totally disoriented.' Kelly liked how Rabbit's horror rose to a new level. How he was there with her. Understanding where she was headed. 'Vivienne couldn't hold on to the conversation. Claimed it was down to a rough time with her previous patient.'

'Kelly, you're saying . . . she played us?'

She stared at the blank space. 'I have no idea. But I think . . . Maybe.'

'She's *one of them*?'

'If so, we've been betrayed in the worst possible way.' She glanced at the kitchen clock. Ten minutes past eight. 'What time is her first appointment?'

'Today, I can't say. But she often starts early enough to meet patients coming off the night shift.'

Kelly started for her bedroom. 'I'll meet you downstairs in five. Bring your weapon.'

FORTY-THREE

Kelly decided to drive and checked out an official car. It would have been faster to walk in early rush-hour traffic, but she intended to make an arrest. Unless, of course, the woman chose to put up a fight. The traffic was moving well, so she did not turn on the lights or siren. No need to let the woman know they were on approach.

Neither she nor Rabbit spoke during the drive. She pulled into a red zone and flipped down the visor to show the Homeland shield. 'Let's move.'

Once in the elevator, Kelly extracted her weapon, checked there was a live round in the chamber, then slipped it back in the holster. She liked how Rabbit did not choose to question her moves. Instead, he simply said, 'I've gone out to the range at least once a week. But I'm still the world's worst shot.'

'It's OK. She'll probably come quietly.' But her training had constantly emphasized the need to be ready for the unexpected. Just as it had stressed the need to stay aware of the risk of subversive influences. Being taken in by the enemy. 'I've been such a total idiot.'

'Vivienne played us like a total pro.' Rabbit's voice carried a harsh tone she had never heard before. 'We came to her at our weakest. She knew it. She *used* us.'

The elevator opened. They walked down the empty hall, Kelly's gun hand down tight to her side. 'Keep behind me.'

She tested the outer door. Kelly was mildly disappointed it wasn't locked. Just then it would have helped to use her rage for something destructive. Like kicking open the door and entering with weapon at the ready.

They entered a silent outer office. Kelly shut the door behind Rabbit. Stopped. Listened carefully.

Silence.

They crossed the waiting room. Then she spotted the note attached to the doorjamb.

TO ALL PATIENTS: I have been called away by a family emergency. My sincere apologies to everyone I was unable to contact. I will be in touch to reschedule . . .

That was as far as Kelly bothered to read.

Kelly entered the therapist's former office, scanned, and gasped.

'What . . .' Rabbit stepped up beside her and spotted it as well. The sound he made was a cough, a gasp, a sob. All rolled into one.

Kelly crossed the room. Rabbit tracked her, a half step behind. Close enough for her to hear his ragged breathing.

She stood looking down, not touching.

Rabbit moved up beside her. Moaned.

Three clear plastic packets rested on the side table next to Vivienne's chair. Each was about an inch square. They held a tiny fleck of something. Scarcely larger than a bit of dust.

The draw.

Kelly had no idea how long she stood there. Minutes. Hours. Eons.

Her phone rang.

She used numb fingers to pull it from her pocket. Focused on the screen. Said, 'It's Agnes.'

Rabbit neither spoke nor moved.

Kelly answered, listened for a moment, then replied, 'I want Rabbit to go with me. And Diyani. Yes, ma'am, both should come. She and Rabbit work as a team in handling input generated by our new group . . . Thank you, ma'am. Rabbit's here with me now. I'll make it clear Diyani can't slow us down. Yes, ma'am. We're leaving now.'

Kelly cut the connection, went back to staring at the untouched packets. 'Agnes wants us to fly down and witness the event. I think we should all see this for ourselves. Determine then if we should . . . you know. If Vivienne's questions are for real. Despite everything.'

Rabbit shuddered his way through a breath, then turned away. 'You take the packets. I can't, I won't . . .'

He staggered from the office.

FORTY-FOUR

Val and Lynda and Reynolds followed Chakkan across the onyx-and-granite-tiled foyer. They passed through the home's three living rooms, then crossed the kitchen and entered a corridor beyond the butler's pantry. The safe rooms were accessed by way of a steel door that belonged on a bank vault.

The sanctuary's central chamber was now home to two make-shift rows of equipment, formed by desks and poker tables and antique sideboards. Stacked along the chamber's other walls were bags, parcels, bales, and boxes rising nearly to the twelve-foot-high ceiling.

Lynda told Chakkan, 'OK, you weren't exaggerating. Bedlam definitely works.'

Sandra rose from her seat by the first line of gear and walked over. 'Somewhere in that pile are sweats and T-shirts, plus thick socks for nights in the true back of beyond.' She smiled at Lynda and continued, 'Connor said to tell you she guessed your size was an eight.'

'That definitely works.'

Sandra waved a hand over the piles. 'Added to that are super-light pallets designed for long-distance trekkers. Cost a fortune. The crates and cloth sacks rimming the kitchen entry hold a ton of fresh produce. The pantry and freezer are both jammed. Ten months' supply of coffee.'

'Hallelujah,' Lynda said.

'Amen to that.' Sandra pretended to notice Reynolds for the first time. 'You're new.'

Chakkan said, 'Somebody needs to talk to Val about picking up strays.'

Val replied, 'Reynolds is not a stray, and I did it because it felt right.'

Sandra said, 'I thought I recognized you. You're Reynolds Hatch.'

'Am I? Oh, good. I was worried.' He unslung the nylon carryall. 'Would it be OK if I filmed?'

Sandra grinned as Chakkan waved arms overhead and stalked back to the first line of equipment. 'Long as the skipper doesn't object.'

'I object to you calling me that! Strenuously!'

Sandra shook Reynolds' proffered hand. 'Bet your ingesting the thread on air rocked all your people behind the camera.'

'They may never recover,' Reynolds said. 'I sure hope my career does.'

'Reynolds is traveling with us far as Grenada,' Val said.

'So, not to Saturn.'

'Not in two billion years,' Reynolds said. 'Joke.'

Chakkan yelled, 'Tick tock, people!'

Sandra started back. 'I believe that's my cue.'

Val stood beside Reynolds and watched the crew of four work the electronic array. 'OK, somebody seal us in,' Chakkan said.

Lynda emerged from the kitchenette, crossed the parlor, and stopped by the control panel. She ran a finger along the line of buttons and toggle switches. Pressed one. The steel door swung silently into place. Three steel bars pressed home. Two lights on the control panel went green. Lynda said, 'Some people might call that overkill.'

The sanctuary's main room was about thirty feet square. The carpet was a silk-and-wool blend that looked and felt expensive. Val thought the storm-grey coloring only added to the chamber's claustrophobic atmosphere.

There were, of course, no windows.

Reynolds unzipped his pack and pulled out a miniature video recorder with built-in mike. He asked Val, 'Can we explore?'

She allowed Reynolds to position her two steps ahead, so he could film her moving around. She paused where he could shoot Chakkan and Sandra and Durrant and Singh working the gear. Then a glance into where Lynda brewed coffee in the cluttered kitchenette. Val passed empty walls where artwork had departed with the former owners. Electronically controlled sliding doors led to bunkrooms, a vast master bedroom, two full baths. More rooms held filtration systems, pumps, generators, air and water tanks, washer and drier, pantry. And a cinema room. Which was when Lynda arrived. She handed them mugs, took in the wall-size screen, the glass-fronted shelving with hundreds and hundreds of DVDs, and declared, 'NASA should be taking notes.'

They returned to the kitchen where Singh and Durrant were using both hands to cradle mugs. Val thought they resembled a pair of frightened rabbits. Smart rabbits, but still.

Sandra joined them. 'We depart the fine community of Bel Air in five minutes, give or take.' She studied the two men, said, 'It's not too late to back out.'

'Yes, it is!' Chakkan waved one arm over his head while not taking his eyes from his monitors. 'Why is the pilot's hand empty?'

Sandra poured another mug, carried it over, returned, and softly addressed the two postdocs. 'Say the word, we can drop you off in Grenada.'

Singh gave the sealed exit a long look, sighed. 'I guess we're good.'

Durrant proved to be made of stronger stuff. He asked his friend, 'Remember where we were this time last year?'

'I remember,' Singh replied.

Durrant told him anyway. 'We were still recovering from being arrested without charges, drugged, and stuck in underground solitary cells.'

Reynolds lifted his eye from the camera, started to speak, but when Val shook her head he went back to filming.

Durrant went on, 'Remember how it felt when Chakkan contacted us? We both thought all this had come full circle. How we were involved in something so great it made everything we'd been through worthwhile.'

Singh said, 'I remember that too.'

Durrant told the others. 'We are here. We are going.'

'Outstanding!' Chakkan called from the main room. 'Sandra, make sure our minions are ready.'

She set down her mug and pulled her phone from her pocket. She hit speed dial, said, 'Wakey-wakey.' To Chakkan, 'We're good to go.'

'Sixty seconds from my mark.'

Sandra passed on the news, then told Durrant, 'Ready the timer.'

The three of them exited the kitchen. Durrant coded in, and a timer appeared on the central console. Frozen at sixty seconds.

'Ready?' Chakkan looked around, then, 'Three, two, one . . . Mark!'

The timer started spinning. The tenths-of-seconds spun in a blur. Fast as Val's heart rate. Finally, it was down to five seconds. Four, three, two, one . . .

Nothing happened.

At least, as far as Val could tell.

Then Sandra leaned back, confirmed, 'Stable at thirty miles.'

Chakkan said, 'Durrant, hit the gas.'

Reynolds cried, 'We're *moving*?'

'Arrival in just under four minutes.'

Reynolds Hatch's response was instantaneous. 'Time for me to play like I know what I'm doing.' He turned to Lynda. 'You mind holding the camera while I talk?'

'Point and shoot, right?' Lynda accepted the miniature gear. 'This is a job I've spent years training for.'

Reynolds positioned two chairs so the lines of equipment formed a background, waited until Val was seated, then said, 'Lynda, step to your left, please, make sure all four scientists are in the background. Are you taping? Perfect. OK, here we go.' He told Val, 'I have four minutes and a thousand questions.'

'You could come with us.' Chakkan spoke without shifting his gaze from the controls. 'Have a little longer with the interview. Say, two weeks give or take.'

'Not on your life.' To Val, 'You intend to travel inside the biggest safe room I've ever seen. Why this choice of vehicle?'

'Back to what I said outside the gates. These three are identical structures, built to exacting standards by the group reputed to be the best in the business.'

Chakkan pulled his chair in tight beside Val and asked Reynolds. 'Mind if I join?'

Reynolds gestured for Lynda to shift over and include Chakkan in the frame. 'By all means.'

Chakkan said, 'Hackers among our group infiltrated the security group's system and identified three of their newest and largest sanctuaries.'

Val said, 'Having them all in the same city helped a lot. We needed to complete the purchases in one day.'

'All three are designed to hold an entire family,' Chakkan said. 'Against what, we have no idea.'

'Zombie apocalypse works for me,' Singh offered.

'Three self-contained habitats,' Val continued. 'Air and water purification systems, power generators with backups, everything required to sustain life inside a totally enclosed environment.'

Sandra leaned away from her controls and offered, 'Some people might question whether life inside a man-made cave is worth the trouble. Three-foot-thick steel-reinforced walls and floors and ceilings, no windows, no way out except through a door made for a bank vault.'

Singh said, 'I'm already getting claustrophobic, and we haven't even started yet.'

'You'll do fine,' Durrant said.

'One of the bathroom closets holds a complete pharmacy,' Sandra told Singh. 'I'm sure there's some kind of happy juice back there.'

'Just what we need,' Durrant said. 'One of our backup pilots getting totally stoned before flying us to Saturn.'

'Speaking of windows,' Reynolds said. 'It seems a shame to go all that way and not see anything.'

'My thoughts exactly,' Durrant said.

'We can change that if we want,' Chakkan said. 'Do we?'

'Yes.' Durrant.

'Maybe.' Singh.

'I vote for seeing Saturn's rings,' Val said. 'Definitely.'

'Could you maybe hold the debate until later?' Reynolds pointed to the spinning digital timer. 'Why three full-scale sanctuaries?'

'Every crucial system in triplicate,' Chakkan replied. 'Except me. I'm irreplaceable.'

'Please insert my big yawn right there,' Sandra said.

'Windows and vision,' Reynolds repeated. 'We've all seen how the bubbles holding the Grenada island and silos are opaque one moment, clear the next.'

Chakkan said, 'We only discovered we could turn the bubbles transparent by accident.'

'By invitation,' Sandra corrected. When Chakkan looked at her, she added, 'You said it first. That's how we're harnessing the dark energy. Inviting it to the party.'

'I was kidding.'

'No, you weren't.'

'Sort of.' To Reynolds, 'The math is crazy complex. Basically, we get the impression this energy is there and waiting.'

'Here, there, everywhere,' Sandra agreed.

'All we have to do is call on it.'

'Invite it in,' Sandra added. 'Like you said.'

'Whatever. We're still on first base when it comes to understanding its potential.'

'Correction,' Singh said. 'We're increasingly certain we can shape it any way we like. The issue is how to translate our request into a form the energy comprehends.'

'Strange as that sounds, it does seem like we're learning a new language, a new manner of communicating across special dimensions,' Sandra agreed.

Reynolds politely insisted, 'Windows. Transparency. Vision.'

'It was our first trip in the plywood rocket,' Chakkan said. 'Then Elizabeth struck.'

'No names,' Sandra said.

'Probably best,' Chakkan agreed. 'One of our top physicists—'

'Who is thankfully not here,' Sandra added.

'Amen to that. So there we were, hanging out at a hundred and twenty thousand feet—'

'Bingo-bango-bongo, the bubble vanished,' Sandra said. 'Sort of.'

'Totally freaked us out,' Chakkan agreed. 'Then we realized, hey, we're still breathing.'

'Once we realized we all weren't going to die, we wanted to murder a certain theoretical physicist and major pain,' Sandra said. 'That was her last time in the plywood rocket.'

Chakkan said, 'The thing is, allowing in visual light also permits all other radiation. Not a good idea in space.'

'But we could do it every now and then.' Durrant did not look up from his monitors. 'Arrival in thirty seconds.'

'I would personally love to see Saturn up close and personal,' Sandra said.

'Last question, then.' Reynolds. 'What else have you learned since the plywood rocket?'

'Lots,' Chakkan said. 'Including how to make and guide bubbles from a distance.' He pointed to where Durrant and Singh worked their equipment. 'Those are our two resident genius experts at long-distance bubbles. After me, of course.'

'You're tops at everything in my book,' Sandra said.

'Why, Sandra. Was that a flirt?'

'No, sweetie. It was me stroking your oversized ego.'

Durrant said, 'Landing in three, two, one.' There was a gentle nudge at floor level. 'Shields merged and we're grounded.'

Singh said, 'The other two sanctuaries are on final approach.' This time the ceiling shook. There was the sound of stone grinding on stone. 'Shields merged. All three sanctuaries are stacked and stable.'

'I hate that word, sanctuary,' Sandra said. 'It sounds like a mausoleum's first cousin.'

They all looked at her. Chakkan said, 'You have an alternative in mind?'

'How about cockpit?'

Smiles all around. Durrant offered, 'Major improvement.'

Singh announced, 'Bubble is transparent. We are now in contact with the outside world. For what it's worth.'

As if in response, Chakkan's phone chimed. He lifted it from the desk and said, 'Grenada Tourism. How may I be of service?' A moment, then, 'Outstanding. Hang on a second.' He checked the room. 'Lynda, could you step over next to the wall? Great.' He said into the phone, 'Ready at this end.'

Sandra said, 'Now you're going to see something cool.'

Reynolds asked Lynda, 'Please tell me you're still recording.'

'You didn't say stop. So I'm still on the job.'

'Pay attention, everyone.' Chakkan pointed at the ceiling. 'Apparently, our miners have been working on molecular realignment for months.'

Singh said, 'They hate being called that. Miners.'

'So they prefer . . .'

'Last I heard, they've been calling themselves couriers,' Sandra replied. 'Plow through three miles of ice. Ring the doorbell. Sign here, please.'

Chakkan nodded. 'That definitely works.'

Sandra explained, 'They're responsible for delivering the nutrients once we arrive.'

Durrant offered, 'Our pals in Canada told the couriers they needed to start working on calculations that could be used for what's about to happen.'

'Molecular realignment, they call it,' Singh said. 'How we work our way through three miles of ice.'

Chakkan pointed to the ceiling. 'Here they come. Lynda, point upward.'

A circle in the roof turned a lighter shade of grey, then started glowing. A greyish fluid began flowing down, slow and treacly. Once it reached the floor, it solidified into a circular staircase with a grey stone banister.

Sandra said, 'Pretty wild, no?'

Singh announced, 'Greg is inbound. Three minutes.'

Chakkan rose to his feet and told Reynolds, 'That's your cue. Unless of course you've changed your mind and want to thumb a ride.'

'Tempting.' Reynolds smiled. 'But thanks just the same. How do I get down?'

Singh said, 'We'll bubble you to a park in Grenada's capital city. Is that a verb, bubble?'

'It is now.' Val walked to the steel portal. 'Are we good?'

Durrant replied, 'Bubble is in place.'

'Wait, please.' Reynolds checked to make sure Lynda was still filming. 'One last word. For everyone who wishes they could come with you. All of us traveling in spirit.'

There was a silence, then Sandra was the one who said, 'I'll go.'

Reynolds motioned to Lynda and said, 'Please do.'

'The closer we come to lift-off,' Sandra said, 'the stronger I'm experiencing a sense of joining.'

'Totally,' Chakkan agreed.

Reynolds nodded. 'It's all too new for me to put into words, but I've been feeling the same.'

'Not with other people, nothing like that,' Sandra continued. 'This is a very unique engagement. With the mission. A purpose. This is redefining the possible. I'm not talking just about the technological advancements that make this trip possible. This is a transition for us as humans. On every level.'

Reynolds walked to Lynda, smiled his thanks, took the camera, re-aimed. 'Val? A word?'

She was ready. 'Two thousand years ago, Julius Caesar crossed the Rubicon River with his army, on their way to conquering Rome and seizing power. Ever since, the word has signified a major transition. Once it has been put in place, there is no going back. The change is irrevocable.' Val paused, then added, 'I'd like to see that as the name of our ship. The Rubicon.'

Reynolds cut off the video, popped out the memory stick. He fished in the shoulder bag, put a fresh one in the machine. He then handed the recorder and a fistful of additional memory sticks to Lynda. 'Keep a record and bring it back, OK?'

'You bet.'

As he crossed to the exit, Chakkan said, 'Do us a favor and tell anybody who's listening we'll be taking off in about an hour.'

'You bet.' Reynolds waited as Val opened the steel portal, glanced inside, then turned back and embraced her. Hard.

He stepped into the bubble, turned back, and said, 'God speed, Rubicon.'

FORTY-FIVE

The Gulfstream's engines whined in readiness as Kelly badged the Andrews Air Base duty officer and was directed to park beside Rabbit's SUV. He and Diyani were already on board when Kelly climbed the jet's stairs. Rabbit was seated next to his wife, gripping her hand and talking intently. Kelly greeted them and took a seat further back, granting the couple what space and privacy she could muster.

Kelly had only flown on a G700 twice before. She liked the jet's size, the luxury, how the acceleration pressed her deep into the leather upholstery. A digital counter was mounted by the cockpit door, and showed both a rapid ascent to 40,000 feet and the jet's swift arrival at maximum cruising speed of Mach .935, well over 1,100 miles per hour. She assumed their destination was the naval air base on Puerto Rico. But the digital clock also had a distance-to-destination counter, and the mileage seemed far too high. She rose and walked up to the cockpit, knocked, entered, and asked, 'Where are you taking us?'

'Our orders are to deliver you to Grenada in no time flat.' The pilot might have been wearing a civvy-style uniform, but his attitude was totally military. 'So we're landing in Barbados. It's a thirty-minute chopper ride from your destination. Cuts well over an hour off your travel time.'

The co-pilot added, 'We're registered as a civilian aircraft, officially flying in from Dulles. No sweat with landing permits.'

The pilot said, 'Your chopper is ready and waiting.'

Kelly thanked them, offered both a coffee, then headed aft. Rabbit and Diyani were still in tight together, heads almost touching as they talked. As Kelly passed, Diyani looked up long enough to shoot Kelly a glance. Kelly thought the woman's incredible eyes resembled molten opals.

Twenty minutes later, Kelly was in the galley making a sandwich when Rabbit walked up. The man had clearly been crying and was still leaking tears. Kelly tried to recall another time when Rabbit had shown such open emotions, and came up with just the one occasion. That awful day when their telepathic abilities had been stripped away.

'Diyani is leaving the decision to me.' He cleared his face with both hands, or tried to. 'You don't know what that means.'

Actually, she had a very good idea. The gift of selfless caring had once been hers to claim. But Kelly remained silent.

'Before we met, her life was all about survival. She lost everything, traveled north with almost nothing . . .' Rabbit breathed hard. Collected himself. 'This telepathic ability, all that's resulted from it and how it brought us together, Diyani had a chance to redefine her life . . .'

Kelly slipped another cup under the Nespresso spout and hit the button. She placed two more slices in the toaster and pretended to watch the machine. The galley fridge was jammed with high-quality items. But everything was already open, and the loaf of sourdough bread was at least a day old. All compliments of the government jet's previous occupants.

'She wants this,' Rabbit managed. 'So much. But she wants us to be stable and happy and permanently together even more.'

The toaster popped. Kelly swiftly put together a second sandwich, set it on a plate, said, 'Diyani takes her coffee black, right?'

'Yes.'

She passed over plate and mug. 'Why don't you take these to her.'

Kelly remained standing in the galley as she ate her sandwich and toasted two more slices. While she prepared Rabbit's meal, she mentally reviewed the man's file. Like a lot of agency analysts, he had been raised in a broken home. Father vanished from the scene when Rabbit was four. Mother remarried twice before Rabbit reached fourteen, but neither man was willing to offer Rabbit the father he needed. Rabbit very much resembled the kid he had once been – highly intelligent, shy, a loner by nature, extremely observant. Scored near genius on the agency's IQ assessments. A CIA analysis cubicle had once seemed a perfect fit.

And look where it had brought him.

Diyani's file made a far more interesting read. Father a farm laborer, mother deceased, brother in the Ecuadorian gangs. He had protected his gifted sister, which allowed her to complete two years of university before he was shot and killed. Diyani fled north, and then in Juarez she met a recruiter. One looking for intelligent migrants, relatively unharmed by the trek. Diyani did not try to refuse. By that point, she was well aware that the recruiter's invitation was in fact no invitation at all. When she was offered the rowan leaf, Diyani took it both because she had no choice and because she was already impacted by its potent draw. The price had been a lifetime of servitude in the drug lord's cadre. Until Rabbit and Kelly and her newly organized crew stormed the drug lord's compound and set them free.

When Rabbit finally returned to the galley, his emotions were back under control. Which was why Kelly had sent him forward. She handed him the sandwich, set another mug in the Nespresso, and said, 'You eat, I'll talk.'

'Should Diyani hear this?'

'She's offered you the space to make your own decision. Let's use it.' When he did not object, she went on, 'One question before we start. Did you ever discuss her entering therapy?'

'Regularly.' He reached for the mug, sipped. 'She wanted to. But she thought one of us at a time was best. She supported me, then later I'd do the same.'

'That is one smart lady.'

'Tell me.'

'So. The leaves.' She patted the pocket to her slacks. 'We all know what we want. The issue isn't desire. It's whether we would be right to accept Vivienne's ultimatum. And for the moment, I think we should assume the choice she offered us was genuine.'

Rabbit said it for her. 'Declare they aren't the enemy. Step across the invisible line.'

She liked how they were moving in tandem. 'At gut level, I think it's a real and valid choice.'

'It moves her subterfuge away from simply spying,' Rabbit said. 'Places it on a level that's more in keeping with the woman I thought I knew. She used the therapy sessions to prepare us for this offer. Right or wrong, she opened us to an alternate perspective.'

But she did not want to talk about Vivienne. Instead, Kelly took her time, laying out her thoughts and observations in sequence. Rabbit finished his sandwich, made another coffee, but otherwise did not move. Kelly was still describing her conversation with Nathan's father when the pilot announced they were six minutes from landing.

All Kelly saw of beautiful Barbados was the ninety feet of sunlit tarmac between the jet and the chopper. They ducked under the spinning rotors and Kelly boarded last. As soon as the door slid shut, the chopper's engines thrummed, and they lifted off.

As they climbed, the sheer scale of activity became increasingly evident. The airport was so jammed with aircraft that the smaller prop planes were parked on the grassy verge. Kelly spotted a 747 bearing the Saudi royal emblem, a metal whale among minnows.

Their ride was a Sikorsky Seahawk, the workhorse of the US naval air fleet. The sky was clear, the sea calm. They followed a ribbon of churned whitewater as broad as a highway and filled with every imaginable type of boat. They passed hundreds of yachts, professional fishing crafts, smaller outboard-motor vessels, and sailboats under power since there was no wind. All of them were headed south by southwest. Same as their chopper and a myriad of other aircraft – private, commercial, military.

Thirty-seven minutes later, they landed on the stern flight deck of the USS Essex, a WASP-class amphibious assault ship. The instant they were clear of the rotors, the chopper revved its engines and took off.

Kelly watched the helicopter maneuver clear of the swarm of fliers circling the island, and felt as if it carried away some part of her own soul. Some past element, a component she once considered vital. And now . . .

She had no idea.

FORTY-SIX

Carlton never slept well on the road and this night was no exception. He ate a room-service breakfast, then sat making notes on work that would fill the coming days. When the clock finally arrived at seven, he left his room and greeted Jadyn with, 'I'm thinking we should cut the trip short.'

'It's the right call.' The head of Terrance's security was as stoic and solid as usual. But the immediacy of his response suggested he'd been thinking the same thing. 'The vice president has been on the phone twice already. Talking to his ladies about what today holds.'

'I was worried,' Carlton confessed. 'Canceling today's appointments might send the wrong signal to all our team.'

'Not a chance,' Jadyn said. 'Nobody is going to pay attention to anything other than our pals leaving Grenada.' He knocked on the door, used his key to unlock it. 'Go make the man's day.'

All the television crews and journalists who had ridden south with them chose to return home by way of the vice president's bus. They shared Terrance's relief at not having to work on a story nobody was interested in. Not that day.

Carlton spent much of the ride with Terrance and Jadyn and the news crews, switching from one television channel to the next, watching and listening with the rest of the world. As they passed Richmond, Carlton shut himself in the rear office and set up a Zoom call with his family. For the first time in what felt like forever, they did not worry about listening ears. Carlton now ran a presidential campaign. Abducting him on legally questionable charges carried minimal risk. Not to mention how the unfolding events erased any benefit their opponents might gain from taking him off the board.

He mostly listened as his wife and daughter gave accounts of Grenada suddenly becoming the center of the entire world's attention. The arrival of six silos, the descent and silent landing of one silvery globe after another, the surge in boat traffic, the rich and famous jetting and yachting in, the diplomats. Even the island's family-run guesthouses were jammed. The Hilton was charging three thousand dollars a night for a single room. Journalists and television crews swarmed. Restaurants stayed open twenty-four seven. People threw money at anyone with a boat. Carlton's wife and daughter pretended to take it all in their stride. But he could see how thrilled they were to be so close to the world-changing action.

Just after midday East Coast time, the three bubbles which had left LA earlier that morning appeared in the sky above the blue-blue Caribbean. The vice president's bus was caught in a massive Beltway traffic jam on its approach to the Foreign Legion Bridge. CBS had been replaying Val's interview by the Bel Air front gates. Carlton thought the young woman handled herself like a pro. Midway through, however, the news anchor interrupted and shifted to where the three large globes descended through the cloud cover. The conference area was completely silent as the softly illuminated bubbles merged with what Carlton was coming to view as the mother ship.

Their bus finally managed the turnoff, joined the Clara Barton Parkway, and picked up speed. Terrance slipped away and called his wife. He resumed his seat as one small globe emerged from the skies and docked, while another separated and flew off in the direction of Grenada. Jadyn was the one who said, 'That's probably Reynolds Hatch.'

When Terrance rejoined the others, he did what Carlton thought was absolutely the right thing and invited the journalists to join them. The unexpected invitation instantly lifted their ride-alongs from the gloom of yet another CBS scoop. Carlton then added the necessary restriction: they must agree to keep Terrance's family out of the story. He doubted very much they would hold to the strict letter of his demand. But it would probably help.

They passed through the Naval Observatory's main gates and were climbing the leafy drive when the CBS announcer suddenly declared they had just been informed the ship would be lifting off in forty-two minutes.

It was the first time Carlton had heard any of the television anchors refer to the massive structure as a spaceship.

Cynthia and Lauren both took the arrival of unexpected guests in stride. The patio table held several large salad bowls, plastic plates and utensils and cups, pitchers of lemonade, mugs and coffee service. Terrance's wife and daughter welcomed the group and brought out the lasagna they had been working on since Terrance had informed them of his return. They gathered in the main parlor and formed a semi-circle around the wall-mounted screen.

They had just finished eating when CBS showed a polished rendition of the video footage Reynolds Hatch shot inside the safe room. Or cockpit, as he called it before and after the airing. Val's calm and somber attitude contrasted remarkably well with the others' lighthearted banter. Twice, Reynolds focused in tight on Val's face. Carlton's heart ached at the prospect of losing that dear, sweet friend.

Their view shifted to an aerial camera showing the three raw concrete structures now stationed atop the silos. The camera zoomed in on the point where a triple line of steel girders ran above the domes. Reynolds supplied a voiceover, explaining these had originally supported the belt-transport system normally used to fill the containers. He reminded the audience of what they had seen when the stairways were formed; moments later, the bottom cockpit's concrete floor began slowly flowing around the I-beams, gripping the steel with what to Carlton looked like stone fists.

When the camera shifted further back and showed the entire ship resting on the rocky island, Lauren declared, 'I'm terrified for them.'

The gathered news people studied her, but to their credit, no one spoke.

Cynthia rose and told her daughter, 'Come help me in the kitchen.'

Carlton and Jadyn both rose as well. Together, they helped clear away the meal's remnants. He could hear Lauren's quietly strident tone, and Cynthia's loving response. Terrance stood as well, then directed the others to remain where they were. As they entered the kitchen, Terrance set his load on the counter, then went back and closed the door. He waited until he was certain his daughter would remain silent, then declared, 'It's time.'

Carlton was glad none of them saw any need to ask what he was talking about.

'Val's words struck me at the deepest level. I want to be part of this transformation. I need this.' Terrance stopped, clearly expecting an objection, warning, urge for caution. When everyone remained silent, he continued, 'This is our future. If I am granted the opportunity, I want to lead from the front line. I *need* this.'

Cynthia was the one who said, 'All right, dear.'

He asked Carlton, 'You agree?'

'It's the right decision,' Carlton replied. 'Taken for the right reasons.'

'Can you make this happen?'

In response, Cynthia crossed the kitchen and opened a carved box by the phone. She extracted a small plastic packet and asked, 'Do you want to wait until all this is over?'

'Now. This very instant.' He looked at his head of security. 'Jadyn, would you go make sure we're not disturbed?'

Jadyn patted the man's arm as he opened the parlor door and stepped out.

Cynthia approached her husband, kissed his cheek, said, 'Hold out your hand.'

FORTY-SEVEN

A young female ensign crossed the flight deck and demanded, 'Which of you is Ms Kaiser?'

'That's me.'

She saluted Kelly. 'Skipper's compliments, ma'am. He's received orders from someplace so high the entire bridge has nose bleeds. What do you need?'

Kelly pointed to the island topped by the six silos and their new concrete crown. 'Can you get us any closer?'

'No problem.' The ensign gestured at a trio of waiting sailors. 'We've got our biggest inflatable ready to power out on your say-so.'

'Any chance you could help us with a change of clothes?' Kelly indicated their Washington attire. 'We got pulled from meetings and flew straight here.'

'Will Navy sweats do?'

'They'd be perfect, thanks.'

'Anything else?'

'A sat phone would help. A lot.'

Ten minutes later, Kelly and Rabbit and Diyani entered the ship's well deck, a hangar-like structure located at the ship's stern waterline. They were settled into the bow seats of a thirty-foot craft powered by twin outboard MerCruisers. They proceeded across the still waters, held to a relatively modest pace by the densely packed vessels.

On close approach, the six silos formed a gargantuan edifice. The massive steel cylinders dominated the island. Far overhead perched the three concrete residences. The globe enclosing the island and silos was utterly transparent. The only way Kelly could be certain it even existed was by watching the craft circling the perimeter, the images wavering slightly as they passed around the protective edge.

The structure looked weirdly out of place, a comical hodgepodge of mismatched pieces. One that dominated the world's attention.

As they approached the clear waters encircling the island, a young petty officer called forward, 'This is as close as we're allowed to come, ma'am.'

'Here is fine.' Kelly passed the sat phone to Rabbit. 'Connect with your team, see if they're picking up anything. Tell them to stay on the line.'

As Rabbit placed the call, the petty officer called, 'Word just came through. The news feeds claim they're five minutes from lift-off.'

As soon as Rabbit's team came on the line, his expression underwent a drastic shift. Shock, yearning, tension, all the words fit. *The draw.*

FORTY-EIGHT

Val was seated in the bottom cockpit's parlor, well removed from the electronic array and their four pilots. She had pulled over one of the swivel chairs that encircled the dining table. The chairs were leather and steel and immensely comfortable. Every time the four pilots reached a momentary pause, they started discussing the option of making windows. She suspected they had already decided, and were just marking time with this endless debate. Val did not mind. The mildly humorous banter kept her from freaking out.

She used a legal pad to begin fashioning the chapters she'd be writing over the coming days. Through the stairwell's opening, she could hear the courier team running through their gear set-up. Lynda was in the kitchen, busy putting together their first meal. Then the sounds of video-game gunfire started emanating from overhead. Chakkan and Sandra looked up from their work. Sandra said, 'Children.'

They resumed the endless circular argument regarding windows, or started to. Then Sandra said, 'You know it's happening.'

'I haven't agreed to anything.'

'You want to watch as much as anybody,' she replied. 'You were born with a double portion of the voyeur gene.'

'I don't even know what that means.'

'Sure you do.' She smiled. 'Skipper.'

Singh laughed without looking up.

Lynda emerged from the kitchen holding a coffee pot and mugs. She handed one to Val and asked, 'You want my opinion?'

'Yes,' Val replied for the group. 'Absolutely. Always.'

'A couple of windows would help settle your crew upstairs.' She used her chin to point at the shouts and gunfire emanating from the floor above. 'Doesn't have to be for long. It also doesn't have to be often. Just the prospect of the occasional glance should be enough.'

'Space radiation causes serious damage,' Chakkan fretted. 'Not to mention how these air systems are probably designed around enclosures of a specific size. We're already taking a risk, linking the units.'

'So seal off the top floor,' Lynda suggested. 'That's your backup section anyway, correct?'

Chakkan glanced at Sandra. 'If I tell the adolescents on the next level to make us some windows, will you promise never to call me skipper ever again?'

'No.'

'Can the decision at least wait until after we lift off?'

'With us losing a chance to watch Earth slip into the starry sky? Don't be silly.'

Chakkan rose in a pretend huff and did his best to stomp toward the stairwell. He yelled through the opening, 'Attention on deck.'

Durrant and Singh and Sandra all laughed.

'Go make yourselves useful and carve us some top-floor viewports.' Chakkan scowled at the cheers and made his way back to his station. 'There. Satisfied?'

'You have earned our undying gratitude, Captain.'

Singh asked, 'Do we salute him?'

Sandra turned back to her work. 'Probably best to give that another day.'

Val marveled at their calm. All of them. The downstairs crew prepping as the digital timer spun down to zero, the couriers upstairs shouting their laughter as they carved holes in their protective space.

Then Sandra announced, 'Three minutes.'

The words released a sudden floodgate of sheer terror. Val was shaken by tremors so hard she dropped the pad. Her fear was a physical assault.

Two billion miles. With this crew.

What if they didn't make it back? A single mistake, a slightly misguided act by one of these totally untrained geeks. And she would be lost to the endless dark, her frozen body spun out into the far reaches, never to . . .

Then it happened.

FORTY-NINE

When they returned to the parlor, Cynthia and Lauren shifted their chairs around. They seated themselves to either side of Terrance, close enough to maintain bodily contact, and took up station holding both his hands. The gathered press watched them, but no one saw a need to speak. Terrance's only indication that something had rocked his internal world was an expression of mild astonishment. Otherwise, he remained as he always was, stoic and calm and resolute.

Carlton wished for a chance to say how proud he was of the man, how honored he was to serve on this campaign . . .

Then it happened.

FIFTY

At one level, Val was aware of the sudden transition inside their cockpit. The utter silence that enveloped the crew, Lynda stepping from the kitchenette, Durrant and Singh turning their chairs so as to stare wide-eyed at Chakkan and Sandra, Greg quietly descending from the upper floor and smiling in Val's direction.

But all this was merely a backdrop to what was *really* happening.

Huge as it was, Val felt none of the overwhelming force she had experienced back in the stone circle, and then again when they connected with Enceladus. This was the same, and yet very different.

From all around the globe, people reached out.

To her.

People she would never meet or truly know. Yet friends just the same. Supporting and encouraging and caring.

There with her.

FIFTY-ONE

The petty officer called forward, 'Ma'am, do we need to worry about a radiation leak?'

'No, you do not.' Kelly kept her gaze fastened upon the immobile Rabbit. 'What just happened?'

Before he could reply, the petty officer called, 'Shouldn't we at least move clear of the blast zone?'

Kelly turned around. 'We are as safe here as we would be on the ship. Count us down to lift-off. Otherwise, I need you to remain silent.' She turned back. 'Tell me.'

The bow held five swivel chairs. Rabbit occupied the central position, Diyani to his left, Kelly to his right. 'Our team says there's some kind of communication. Or joining together. They say it's like listening to a global chorus.'

On his other side, Diyani softly moaned.

'All the telepaths, everywhere on Earth, they've come together. They're saying farewell to their people on the ship.'

'I want to be part of this.' Diyani almost sang the words. 'So much.'

The petty officer called, 'Sixty seconds.'

Kelly took the three packets from the pocket of her sweats. Held them low, her hand resting on her thigh.

Rabbit's expression turned pinched, almost feral. 'There is no danger here. From these people. Their new abilities. The rowan. What it offers.'

Kelly felt an idea take hold. One so potent her entire body vibrated in utter resonance.

'There never was!' Rabbit pointed across the empty waters. 'They're not the enemy!'

The petty officer called, 'Twenty seconds.'

'We were wrong,' Rabbit said. 'All this time, what we did . . .'

He reached over and took the two packets.

This time, Diyani's lyrical moan resonated in time to Kelly's own tremors.

'Five seconds! Four, three, two . . .'

While all the world's attention was elsewhere, Rabbit handed one packet to Diyani. Instantly, their hands became filled with illuminated threads. Together they lifted, breathed . . .

'There they go!'

Silently, with incredible grace for such an awkward structure, the silos lifted free. Kelly's craft became surrounded by shouts and screams and blaring horns. From the globe itself, however, there was no sound at all.

'Ma'am, are your mates all right? They're glowing!'

Kelly's only response was to slip her own packet back out of sight.

Rabbit looked at her, astounded. 'You're not doing this?'

The draw was so immense that Kelly had no room for words. She rose to her feet, stepped further toward the bow, and stood there. Her body still vibrated in resonance to her decision. And the thwarted desire.

And with remorse over all the wrong moves.

When the spacecraft was lost to the now-empty sky, Kelly told the petty officer, 'Take us back to the ship.'

FIFTY-TWO

In the end, the miners or couriers or whatever they wanted to be called set up the top structure's roof as an observation deck.

Between the middle and top units they put in a double-door enclosure, sealing the stairwell at the top and the bottom. Ditto between the top floor and the roof.

On the roof they added benches, railings, a picnic table no one would ever use, even a couple of concrete sunchairs to catch the faint of heart.

Once they cleared the island, everyone but Durrant trooped upstairs. The postdoc volunteered to stay on duty, explaining how the thought of watching his home planet shrink away left him ready to hurl.

Val thought the couriers looked and acted like a cluster of hyper-excited teens. She gave their antics ten seconds, then turned her attention to . . .

Earth.

She was vaguely aware of Greg Alderton stepping up beside her. The pale young man sniffed softly, then released one hand from the railing long enough to wipe his face. Val found herself glad at least one of them was able to weep. Whether it was in farewell or appreciation of the beauty on display hardly mattered.

They were already high enough for Val to see the world's curvature. Directly beneath them, the swiftly shrinking Caribbean shone like liquid sapphire holding solid green gemstones. The largest yachts were already the size of ants. Another breath and they were lost entirely. They moved higher still, and the atmospheric blanket glowed a soft veiled white.

Val was suddenly gripped by a gasping, clenching terror.

In response, Greg placed one hand on top of hers. In that same moment, the global chorus of unseen friends soothed her heart and mind.

Greg asked, 'All right?'

'Yes.' And it was.

'That's it, show's over.' Chakkan clapped his hands. 'We need to fully raise the shields.'

The couriers responded like disappointed children. Moaning and complaining it wasn't nearly long enough.

But Chakkan was already taking the stairs. 'We're approaching Low Earth Orbit. Beyond that, space radiation causes increased risk of cancer. Central nervous system damage. Degenerative diseases. Everything we definitely want to avoid.'

Val and Greg and Lynda and Singh and Sandra all started for the stairwell, leaving the couriers begging for one minute more.

As she started her descent, Val paused long enough for a final look up, taking in how the stars grew ever more brilliant.

Then she went below. Ready to depart.

And determined to make it home.

FIFTY-THREE

Kelly gave it seven days.

Her timing mostly came down to Rabbit's departure. Which he and Diyani managed to keep very quiet, very contained.

Rabbit was of course aided by the near-frantic state dominating everyone even remotely connected to the White House. During that same seven-day period, Agnes and Avri Rowe and General Skarren all developed haggard features from severe sleep deprivation. Four times during that period, Agnes requested a sit-rep from Rabbit's team. Each time, he responded the same way: that since the craft's departure everything and everyone had gone quiet. Kelly waited to see if Agnes questioned this. But each time, she merely ordered them to issue an alert the instant anything changed, then moved on. After all, Kelly's superiors had more pressing matters to worry about.

The president's re-election campaign was, in a word, unraveling.

The president and his team wanted to talk about the economy, jobs report, inflation, foreign policy, anything except the spaceship and the global movement his administration had supposedly sought to eradicate. Which was all the press was interested in discussing.

The congressional inquiry continued to gather steam.

Six days after lift-off, two new polls were released. Both showed Vice President Terrance Dale with a commanding lead.

That was the same morning Kelly's team discovered that Rabbit and Diyani and all their crew had vanished.

The first they knew of something amiss was when one of Barry's team showed up for duty and reported the front desk was empty. An inspection of the security camera feeds showed how half an hour earlier, at four thirty in the morning, all of Rabbit's crew simply filed out and climbed into a bus idling at the curb.

The last persons out were the young woman on night duty and Rabbit, who thoughtfully locked the front door before boarding.

Just as the morning news reports announced the poll results, Kelly and her superiors received a one-sentence email from Rabbit, announcing their resignation. Effective immediately, signed by each team member.

The next morning, day seven since lift-off, Kelly knew it was time.

Darren easily found the address for her. Kelly had an excuse ready, that she'd mistakenly deleted the text containing the address change, but Darren did not question her request.

The drive to Tyson's Corner took eighteen minutes, not bad in early rush hour. Her destination was the high-rent executive office building on Tyson Boulevard. It was a good location for someone wanting to vet all new arrivals. Kelly was required to give her name twice, first to enter the underground parking garage and again at the ground-floor security desk. Only when the guard phoned upstairs for approval was Kelly allowed to enter the elevator lobby. She had no problem with being announced. It made as clear a statement as possible about her intent.

Vivienne Grace was standing by her open door when Kelly arrived. Arms tight across her chest. Face pinched. But there.

Kelly stepped up and waited while Vivienne searched her face. Finally, the therapist re-entered her waiting room, pausing only long enough to address the man standing by the window, 'This will only take a moment, Stefan.'

The man shot Kelly a hard look, then went back to texting. He shifted his weight enough to open his jacket and reveal a gold badge attached to his belt.

Vivienne's new office was set up in a nearly identical format to her former digs. Beige translucent drapes filtered the sunlight and cast the room in soft comforting tones. Vivienne crossed to her desk, then leaned against the corner. Crossed her arms again. Waiting.

Kelly held out the small packet. 'Your tactics were abysmal. Borderline illegal. But I'm moving beyond all that because I have to. Your message was correct. Your motives were right. This group is not the enemy and never was.' She watched Vivienne take an easier breath and relax a fraction. 'So here's what's going to happen. As far as everyone on Earth is concerned, I am still part of the team run by the White House. On the surface, my remit stays the same.'

Vivienne uncrossed her arms. Opened her mouth. But whatever she wanted to say remained unspoken.

Kelly asked, 'The inability to read thoughts – has that changed?'

'I . . . No. Not yet.' Her voice had taken on an unsteady note. 'But I can't say where all this is headed.'

'Understood.' Kelly was mildly pleased to shake this woman's world. 'As far as everyone else is concerned, including all of the others linked up, you and I are still therapist and patient. Agreed?'

'Yes. Definitely.' Stronger this time.

'OK. Good.' Kelly took a long breath.

Then, finally, at long last . . .

She gave in to the draw.